NADIRS

Nadirs

(Niederungen)

Herta Müller

Translated and
with an afterword
by Sieglinde Lug

University of Nebraska Press
Lincoln

Publication of this translation was
assisted by a grant from Inter Nationes
Herta Müller, Niederungen © 1988 Rotbuch Verlag, Berlin
Translation and afterword © 1999 by
the University of Nebraska Press
Library of Congress Cataloging-in-Publication Data
Müller, Herta.
[Niederungen, English]
Nadirs (Niederungen) / Herta Müller ; translated and with
an afterword by Sieglinde Lug.
p.   cm. – (European women writers series)
ISBN 0-8032-3197-0 (cl.: alk. paper). –
ISBN 0-8032-8254-0 (pbk.: alk. paper)
I. Lug, Sieglinde.   II. Title.   III. Series.
PT2673.U29234N5413   1999
833'.914 – dc21
98-48347
CIP

CONTENTS

NADIRS

THE FUNERAL SERMON

At the railway station, relatives were running alongside the puffing train. With every step they moved their raised arms and waved.

A young man was standing behind a window of the train. The glass reached up to his armpits. He was clutching a bunch of tattered white flowers to his chest. His face was rigid.

A young woman was carrying a bland child out of the railway station. The woman was a hunchback.

The train was leaving for the war.

I turned off the television.

Father was lying in a coffin in the middle of the room. The walls were covered with so many pictures that you couldn't see the wall.

In one picture, Father was half as tall as the chair he was holding onto.

He was wearing a dress and his bowed legs were all rolls of fat. His head was pear-shaped and bald.

In another picture Father was the bridegroom. You could see only half of his chest. The other half was a bunch of tattered white flowers in Mother's hands. Their heads were so close together that their earlobes were touching.

In a different picture Father was standing bolt upright in front of a fence. There was snow under his boots. The snow was so white that Father was surrounded by emptiness. His hand was raised above his head in a salute. There were runes on his collar.

In the picture next to it, Father had a hoe resting on his shoulder. Behind him there was a cornstalk sticking up into the sky. Father was wearing a hat on his head. His hat cast a wide shadow and hid his face.

In the next picture, Father was sitting behind the steering wheel of a truck. The truck was full of cows. Every week Father would drive the cows to the slaughterhouse in the city. Father's face was thin and had hard edges.

In all the pictures, Father was frozen in the middle of a gesture. In all the pictures, Father looked as though he didn't know what to do. But Father always knew what to do. That's why all these pictures were wrong. All those false pictures, all those false faces chilled the room. I wanted to get up from my chair, but my dress was frozen to the wood. My dress was transparent and black. It crackled whenever I moved. I rose and touched Father's face. It was colder than the objects in the room. It was summer outside. Flies were dropping their maggots in flight. The village stretched along the wide sandy road. The road was hot and brown, and burned out your eyes with its glare.

The cemetery was made of rocks. There were boulders on the graves.

When I looked down on the ground I noticed that the soles of my shoes were turned up. All that time, I had been walking on my shoelaces. Long and heavy, they were lying behind me, their ends curled up.

Two staggering little men were lifting the coffin from the hearse and lowering it into the grave with two tattered ropes. The coffin was swinging. Their arms and their ropes got longer and longer. The grave was filled with water despite the drought.

Your father killed a lot of people, one of the drunk little men said.

I said: he was in the war. For every twenty-five killed he got a medal. He brought home several medals.

He raped a woman in a turnip field, the little man said. Together with four other soldiers. Your father stuck a turnip between her legs. When we left she was bleeding. She was Russian. For weeks afterwards, we would call all weapons turnips.

It was late fall, the little man said. The turnip leaves were black and folded over by frost. Then the little man put a big rock on the coffin.

The other drunk little man continued:

For the New Year, we went to the opera in a small German town. The singer's voice was as piercing as the Russian woman's screams. One after the other, we left the theater. Your father stayed till the end. For weeks afterwards, he called all songs turnips and all women turnips.

The little man was drinking schnapps. His stomach was gurgling. There is as much schnapps in my belly as there is ground water in the graves, the little man said.

Then the little man put a big rock on the coffin.

The man giving the funeral sermon was standing next to a white marble crucifix. He came toward me. He had his two hands buried in his coat pockets.

The man giving the funeral sermon had a rose the size of a hand in his button hole. It was velvety. When he was right next to me he pulled one hand out of his pocket. It was a fist. He wanted to straighten out his fingers but wasn't able to. The pain made his eyes bulge. He began crying quietly to himself.

In the war, you can't get along with your countrymen, he said. You can't order them around.

Then the man giving the funeral sermon put a big rock on the coffin.

Now a fat man came and stood next to me. His head was like a tube without a face.

Your father slept with my wife for years, he said. He blackmailed me when I was drunk and stole my money.

He sat down on a rock.

Then a scrawny wrinkled woman came toward me, spat on the ground, and cursed me.

The funeral congregation was standing at the opposite end of the grave. I looked down at myself and was startled because they could see my breasts. I felt cold.

Everybody's eyes were on me. They looked empty. Their pupils were stabbing from under their lids. The men carried guns over their shoulders, and the women were rattling their rosaries.

The man giving the funeral sermon was plucking at his rose. He tore off a blood-red petal and ate it.

He signaled me with his hand. I knew that now I had to give a speech. Everybody was looking at me.

I couldn't think of a single word. My eyes were rising to my head through my throat. I put my hand to my mouth and gnawed at my fingers. You could see my teethmarks on the backs of my hands. My teeth were hot. Blood was running from the corners of my mouth onto my shoulders.

The wind had torn a sleeve off my dress. It was hovering black and billowing in the air.

A man was leaning his cane against a big rock. He aimed his rifle and shot down the sleeve. When it sank to the ground in front of me it was covered with blood. The funeral congregation applauded.

My arm was naked. I felt it petrify in the air.

The speaker gave a signal. The applause stopped.

We are proud of our community. Our achievements save us from decline. We will not let ourselves be insulted, he said. We will not let ourselves be slandered. In the name of our German community you are condemned to death.

They all pointed their guns at me. There was a deafening bang in my head.

I fell over and didn't reach the ground. I lay suspended in the air across their heads. Quietly I pushed open the doors.

My mother had cleared all the rooms.

Now there was a long table in the room where the body had been laid out. It was a butcher's table. There was an empty white plate and a vase with a bunch of tattered white flowers on it.

Mother was wearing a transparent black dress. She was holding a big knife in her hand. Mother stood in front of the mirror and cut off her heavy gray braid with the big knife. She carried the braid to the table with both hands. She put one end on the plate.

I will wear black for the rest of my life, she said.

She set fire to one end of the braid. It reached from one end of the table to the other. The braid burned like a fuse. The fire was licking and devouring.

In Russia they shaved off my hair. That was the least punishment, she said. I staggered with hunger. At night I crawled into a turnip field. The guard had a gun. If he had seen me he would have killed me. The field didn't rustle. It was late fall and the turnip leaves were black and folded over by frost.

I didn't see Mother any more. The braid kept burning. The room was filled with smoke.

They killed you, my mother said.

We couldn't see each other any more, there was so much smoke in the room.

I heard her footsteps close to me. I was groping for her with outstretched arms.

Suddenly she hooked her bony hand into my hair. She shook my head. I screamed.

I suddenly opened my eyes. The room was spinning around. I was lying in a ball of tattered white flowers and was locked in.

Then I had the feeling that the apartment building was tipping over and emptying itself into the ground.

The alarm clock rang. It was Saturday morning, five-thirty.

THE SWABIAN BATH

It is Saturday night. The bath stove has a glowing belly. The ventilation window is shut tight. Last week two-year-old Arni caught a cold from the chilly air. Mother is washing little Arni's back with faded panties. Little Arni is thrashing about. Mother lifts little Arni out of the bathtub. Poor child, says Grandpa. Such young children shouldn't be given a bath, says Grandma. Mother climbs into the bathtub. The water is still hot. The soap is foaming. Mother is rubbing little gray rolls off her neck. Mother's rolls are floating on the surface of the water. The tub has a yellow ring. Mother climbs out of the bathtub. The water is still hot, Mother calls to Father. Father gets into the bathtub. The water is warm. The soap is foaming. Father is rubbing little gray rolls off his chest. Father's rolls are floating with Mother's rolls on the surface of the water. The tub has a brown ring. Father gets out of the bathtub. The water is still hot, Father shouts to Grandma. Grandma gets into the bathtub. The water is lukewarm. The soap is foaming. Grandma is rubbing little gray rolls off her shoulders. Grandma's rolls are floating with Mother's and Father's rolls on the surface of the water. The tub has a black ring. Grandma gets out of the bathtub. The water is still hot, Grandma shouts to Grandpa. Grandpa gets into the bathtub. The water is ice cold. The soap is foaming. Grandpa is rubbing little gray rolls off his elbows. Grandpa's rolls are floating with Mother's, Father's, and Grandma's rolls on the surface of the water. Grandma opens the bathroom door. Grandma looks into the bathtub. Grandma can't see Grandpa. The black bathwater is sloshing over the black rim of the bathtub. Grandpa must be in the bathtub, Grandma thinks. Grandma closes the bathroom door behind her. Grandpa drains the bathwater from the bathtub. The little gray rolls of Mother, of Father, of Grandma, and of Grandpa are whirling around the drain.

The Swabian family, freshly bathed, is sitting in front of the TV. The Swabian family, freshly bathed, is waiting for the Saturday night movie.

MY FAMILY

My mother is a muffled woman.

My grandmother is blind with cataracts. In one eye she has the gray cataract, in the other a green cataract.[*]

My grandfather has a scrotal hernia.

My father has another child with another woman. I don't know the other woman and the other child. The other child is older than I am, and that's why people say I was fathered by a different man.

My father gives Christmas presents to the other child and tells my mother that the other child was fathered by a different man.

For New Year's, the postman always brings me one hundred lei[†] in an envelope and says it's from Santa Claus. But my mother says that I am not the child of another man.

People say that my grandmother married my grandfather because he owned a field and that she was in love with another man and that it would have been better if she had married the other man because she is so closely related to my grandfather that it is just plain incest.

Other people say that my mother is by a different man and that my uncle is by a different man, not by the same different man, but by another one.

---

[*]The German word for cataract is "star," meaning "starling"; the different cataracts are then called by the bird's colors, gray and green.
[†]Romanian currency.

That's why the grandfather of another child is my grandfather, and people say that my grandfather is the grandfather of another child, though not of the same different child, but of another one. And they say that my great-grandmother died very young of a supposed cold, and that it was something entirely different from natural death, namely suicide.

And other people say that it was something different from sickness and something different from suicide, namely murder.

After her death, my great-grandfather immediately married another woman. She already had a child by another man to whom she was not married, yet she was married at that time. And after this other marriage, she had another child with my great-grandfather. People say that this other child is also by a different man, not by my great-grandfather.

Every Saturday, year after year, my great-grandfather would go to a small town that was a health spa.

People say that in this small town he had relations with another woman.

He was even seen in public holding another child's hand, even speaking a different language with that child.

He was never seen with the other woman, but people say that she couldn't have been anything but a resort whore since my great-grandfather never accompanied her in public.

People say that a man who has another woman and another child outside his village has to be despised and that it is no better than incest, that it is even worse than outright incest, that it is an outright disgrace.

NADIRS

Purple blossoms next to fences, marigold with its greenish fruit between the children's baby teeth.

Grandfather said that marigold leaves make you stupid, you mustn't eat them. And you don't want to be stupid now, do you.

The bug that crawled into my ear. Grandfather poured alcohol into my ear so that the bug wouldn't crawl into my head. I cried. There was a buzz in my head and it got hot. The whole yard was whirling around, and Grandfather was standing in the middle like a giant, whirling with it.

You have to do this, Grandfather said, otherwise the bug will crawl into your head, and then you'll be stupid. And you don't want to be stupid now, do you. Acacia blossoms in the village roads. The snowed-in village with the bee colonies in the valley. I ate acacia blossoms. They had a sweet stem inside. I chewed one and kept it in my mouth for a long time. As I swallowed it I already had the next blossom between my lips. There were countless blossoms in the village, you couldn't eat all of them. Every year all those big trees would bloom.

You mustn't eat acacia blossoms, Grandfather said, there are little black flies in them and if they crawl into your throat that'll strike you dumb. And you don't want to be dumb now, do you.

The long alley with its wild vine, the ink-colored grapes cooking in the sun under their delicate skin. I bake sand pies, I grind bricks into red paprika, I scrape the skin off my wrists. It burns in my bones.

Dolls made of corn with braids. Hair made of cornsilk feels cool and brittle. In the barns we play mother and father, in the straw we lie next to each other and on top of each other. Our clothes are between us. Sometimes we take off our stockings, and the straw pokes into our legs. We put our stockings on again furtively, and then there is straw on our skins when we walk. It scratches our feet.

Every day we have babies, corncob children in the henhouse, doll children on the chicken ladder. Their dresses flap when the wind comes through the boards.

Kittens are bundled up in dolls' clothes, tied down in the cradle and rocked to sleep. I sing lullabies and rock the cats until they are dizzy. And their fur bristles under their clothes. And their eyes get dull and big, and then saliva and curdled puke runs from their mouths.

Grandfather cuts their strings and lets them go. For a while they stagger, then their fur gets smooth again, but they still walk through emptiness, without putting their paws down, without living, they look deep into the summer.

Butterflies rise from the grapevine and dance across the yard.

We hunt cabbage butterflies that have fragile veins in their wings. We wait for them to scream when we impale them on a pin, but they don't have a bone in their bodies, they are light and can do nothing but fly, and that's not enough when the summer is everywhere.

They flutter themselves to death on the pins.

In Swabian dialect they call an animal corpse a carcass. A butterfly can't be a carcass. It falls apart without decomposing.

Flies in the washbowl, drowned mad ventilator hum in the sour milk bucket. Flies on the soapy gray surface of the water in the washbowl. Bulging eyes, extended pricks piercing the water, frantic spindly little legs.

Soon they twitch for the last time, remaining on the surface, lighter and lighter with so much death.

Two drops of blood per butterfly get stuck under my fingernails. The torn-off head of the fly falls from my hand to the ground like a weed seed.

Grandfather let us play.

The swallows are the only ones you have to let live, they are useful birds, he said. And the word vermin is for cabbage butterflies and carcass is for all those dead dogs.

Caterpillars which are actually butterflies crawl out of their cocoons. Cocoons, fake cotton sticking to the vine stakes.

And where did the first butterfly come from, Grandfather? And leave me alone with your stupid questions, nobody knows that, just go and play.

Our dolls that sleep in clean starched dresses on the beds of uninhabited bedrooms.

Ever since Mother's wedding night nobody has breathed in these beds.

And that night we were so tired that your father after throwing up in the bathroom fell asleep immediately. He didn't touch me that night, Mother said and giggled and then was silent.

It was May, and that year we had cherries already. Spring had arrived early.

We went to pick the cherries ourselves, your father and me. And then while picking cherries we had a fight, so we didn't speak a word all the way home. Your father didn't touch me while we were picking cherries in the large deserted vineyard either. He was standing next to me like a pole and spitting out wet slithery pits, and I knew then that he would beat me often in our life together.

When we came home the women in the village had baked whole baskets full of cake, and the men had slaughtered a young beautiful cow. The hoofs were on the manure pile. I saw them when I came through the gate and entered the yard.

I went to cry in the attic so that nobody would see me, so that nobody would find out that I wasn't a happy bride.

At the time I wanted to say I don't want to get married, but I saw the slaughtered cow, and Grandfather would have killed me.

A cough shakes Mother's head and sprays spit from her mouth. Her neck gets all wrinkled in the process. It is short and heavy. At one time, I assume, it must have been beautiful, at one time before I existed.

Ever since I was born my mother's breasts have been sagging, ever since I was born Mother has had bad legs, ever since I was born Mother has had a drooping belly, ever since I was born Mother has had hemorrhoids and moans in agony in the bathroom.

Ever since I was born Mother has talked about my gratitude as a child and started crying and scratching the fingernails on one hand with the fingernails of the other hand. Her fingers are cracked and hard.

Only when she counts money are they smooth and limber like spiders spinning a thread.

Mother keeps the money in the bedroom in the pipe of the tiled stove. Father always demands money when he wants to buy anything. He wants to buy something every day and demands money every day because everything costs money. And every night Mother asks him what he did with the money, what on earth did he do with all that money.

When Mother goes to get the money she doesn't pull up the blinds on the windows. In the middle of the day she turns on the light in the room, and the lamp with its five arms emits light from one single dim bulb. The other four arms are dead.

Mother counts the money out loud so she can take it in better with her hands and her eyes. She keeps counting one-hundred-lei bills and spits from time to time on her fingertips.

Her hands are cracked and in the summer they are as green as the plants she handles.

On spring nights Mother comes home from weeding thistles and brings me sorrel in her pocket and in the summer a huge sunflower.

I stand in the backyard and eat the seeds with the chickens. While doing that I think of the fairy tale where the girl always feeds her animals first and only after that does she eat. And later the girl becomes a princess and all the animals love her and help her. And one day a handsome blond prince marries her. And they are the happiest couple far and wide.

The chickens had eaten up all the seeds and were looking at the sun with cocked heads. The sunflower was empty. I broke it into pieces. Inside there was white spongy pulp that was itchy on my hands.

If a bee flies into your mouth you die. It stings your gums. The gums swell up so big that you suffocate on your own gums, Grandfather said. While I picked flowers I constantly thought of not opening my mouth. But sometimes I felt like singing. I clenched my teeth and squashed the song. My lips would hum and I looked around me to see if it wasn't precisely my humming that would bring a bee to me. There wasn't a bee to be seen far and wide.

But I wanted one to come. And I will keep humming and show it that it can't fly into my mouth.

Two stiff braids sticking out sideways. Two bows braided into them.

Reeds, torn down to the roots, white with rough reddish veins that turn dark red at the ends and grow out of the reeds and dissolve into nothing.

The reeds get torn to shreds till they look like hair. My beautiful corn doll, my good child, dumb, without a neck, without arms, without legs, without hands, without a face.

I cut out two kernels of corn. The coarse cob looks out of the holes with a faraway gaze. I cut out three kernels next to each other and three below each other. I look at the rigid mouth and the poked-out nose.

A doll with a hard bulky face. When it falls to the ground, when it dries out, seeds keep falling from its body and it will have a hole in its belly or three eyes or a big scar on its nose or cheek or it will have chewed-up lips.

The stalks of grass are shredded to the point of transparency. If you look through them you can see that the summer is fragile.

From the fields you see the village as a herd of houses grazing between the hills and you can determine the kinds of vegetation only by their colors. Everything seems close, and if you go toward it you never reach it. I have never understood these distances. I was always behind, everything ran ahead of me. There was only dust in my face. And no end in sight.

When you leave the village you meet the crows who peck into space from time to time.

Further down in the valley, in the gray powder of the dirt road there are dog roses with sunstrokes in their red heads. And next to them the sloes remain blue and cool. Their leaves are smeared with the chalky shit of songbirds.

They always sing the same song. When they are gone the singing stops, and all that remains is the same chalky shit everywhere.

You can't hear the songbirds in the village, they don't come to the houses because there are so many cats in the village, most of them from around the whole region. And there are as many dogs in the village as there are cats. The dogs drag their bellies through the grass and on their way they dribble piss that is warm from their bodies. They are small and their coats are scraggly.

Their small pointed heads wiggle when they walk and watery expressionless birds' eyes roll in them. There is always fear in those dogs' eyes, in those dogs' skulls. The dogs get kicked by both men and women. But the women's kicks are not as harsh because of the shoes they wear.

The men wear these hard boots. Their feet are stuck in them to their tops, and heavy rough laces are strapped over the tongues.

Those kicks kill the dogs instantly, and then they lie there next to the roads for days, bent or stretched out and stiff and stinking under a swarm of flies.

Leaf atrophy flies through the air like invisible fungi.

And when the fruit trees get sick the men in the village say that that damned fungus from the forest is back. They mix their bright green poisonous insecticides that form bubbles on the leaves and burn the nerves. The leaves end up rough and pitted like sieves. And the spiders tie their white spit webs on the abused edges.

The mud has turned green with algae.

Flies buzz through the greasy feathers of the geese.

When the rain that makes the wood rot in the summer soaks the soil, you can see how deep the roads are and how washed out the soil is.

Then the cows wear big shapeless shoes of mud they bring through the doors of the houses. You can smell the grass in their bellies. The lumps of grass that rise in their throats again after their first chewing hurt me deep in my chest. The cows chew absent-mindedly and their eyes are drunk with all that grazing. Every night they come back to the village with those drunk eyes.

Once our cow took me on her horns and jumped over a ditch with me. Then she dropped me in a deep rut and rushed over me. Her dung-splattered teats seemed to get torn off in the process.

I followed her with my eyes. Hot air blew after her for a while. My flesh was burning where the skin was scraped off my knees, and I was afraid that I couldn't be alive any more with so much pain, and at the same time I knew that I was still alive because it hurt. I was afraid that death would find its way into me through this open knee and I quickly covered my wounds with my hands.

And since I was still alive I was overcome with hate.

I wanted to pierce her big hairy belly with my eyes, dig into her hot bowels with my hands, grab her under her skin up to my elbows.

The cranesbill still had yesterday's rain in its scratchy leaves. I washed my face with the brown water, and in the evening I had really red cheeks and in the mirror I saw how I was getting more and more beautiful.

And when I drove the cow down into the valley with my hatred I looked for the biggest cranesbill plant in the whole valley. As the cow was lowering its square head into the grass and the bony frame of her butt was right next to me, I got undressed to the skin and washed my whole body this time. The cow had turned towards me and her eyes were unbearably large. Her gaze gave me goose-bumps. Even the cranesbill plant was shaking itself and grew bigger and bigger and more and more scratchy. So I quickly put on my clothes again.

When my skin got dry it tightened and felt like glass. My whole body felt how I was getting beautiful and I stepped carefully not to break apart. The grass blades fanned out with supple grace as if moved by my gait and I was afraid they would cut me. My gait had something of my grandmother's starched linen. When I slept in it the first night it rustled with any move, and I believed my skin was rustling.

Sometimes I would lie very quietly and yet it would rustle. And I was afraid that the big bony man was in my room, the one who had bought a house on the edge of the village, and no one knew where he had come from, and everybody knew that he didn't have to work because he had sold his huge skeleton to the museum and got a monthly income from that.

That man was in my room for entire nights. I kept seeing him behind the curtain, under the bed, behind the closet, in the tiled stove.

At night when fear scared off my sleep, when I got up and groped around the furniture in the dark and didn't find him I still knew he was there.

In the morning all I found was brown dusty moths on the ceiling, they would hit the lampshade at night.

I touched them. My fingers were covered with brown dust, and where I touched them their wings became transparent. When I let the moths go they were still fluttering around under my knee for a while. They couldn't make it any higher, and I stepped on them with my shoe to deliver them from their pain. Their velvety bulging bellies popped and sprinkled white milk on the floor. Then loathing crawled up on me from my shoes and put its tentacles around my throat, and its hands were gaunt and cold like the hands of the old people I saw in those beds with lids in front of which people would sit in silence and prayer.

The old women's chins would tremble above the stiff knots in their scarves. I saw the slime on their sparse wet eyelashes and didn't understand the meaning of their tears.

Grandmother said that these beds were coffins and she said those lying in them were dead. And when she said that she thought that I wouldn't understand the word. I understood it without ever having heard it. For days I carried it around with me and I saw a corpse in every piece of chicken in the soup, and Grandmother didn't take me to the dead any more.

But when there was music in the village on a weekday afternoon I knew that someone had died again.

I didn't understand why dying always happened behind the walls of the houses and you could never see it except when it was finished even if you lived next door your whole life.

Once a man died in the open field. Lightning had struck him. He was the first husband of the woman who then married her brother-in-law who then died of a lung disease; and then she remained alone for years because nobody would marry her any more; and her son, who resembled the ragman who came through the village in the summer, had a bushel of gray hair under his temple like nobody in the village; when her son was grown up she married a man from a neighboring village who is still alive and who had to carry his own child to baptism because nobody wanted to be his godfather since everybody believed that death would get you too if you touched this woman's child.

Later when I came to the city I did see dying in the streets before it was finished.

People would fall on the asphalt, whimper, twitch, and they didn't belong with anyone. And then there were people who took their rings and their watches as long as their hands weren't quite stiff yet and they tore gold necklaces from women's necks and earrings from their ears. Their earlobes would tear and soon stop bleeding.

Once I was alone with a dead stranger. And after I had looked at him much too long I ran crying to the first streetcar I saw to take me to a part of the city unknown to me. At the last station the conductor made me get off next to a tree.

On my way back all the streets were blocked off by thick walls.

I looked up at the apartment houses as if I was at the bottom of a canyon and said to myself that in my village people aren't lying in the streets but in beds with lids, and people sit and pray in front of them.

And they keep those dead people in the house for a long time. Only when their ears start turning green on the edges from decomposing do people stop crying and carry them out of the village.

And they say that the most recently deceased person guards the cemetery until the next one dies.

Squealing salamanders in a nest that resembles a handful of frazzled corn fibers. Glued-shut eyes ooze from every naked mouse. Thin little legs like wet thread. Crooked toes.

Dust trickles down from wooden planks.

You get chalky fingers from it, and it settles on the skin of your face so that you get the feeling of being dried out.

Baskets, woven of willow, with two handles that cut into your hands. Calluses grow in your palms and blisters, hot and hard, pain throbbing through them.

The old mice are gray and padded as if they had been petted all their lives. They are running back and forth without making a sound and drag long round strings behind them. And their heads are so small that it seems they have to see everything pointed and small and flat from such a skull.

Look how much damage they do, says Mother. All the chaff down there was once corn, and they ate all of it.

A nose pokes out from under a corn cob, then two eyes twitch. Mother has a corn cob ready in her hand. The blow gets the head. There is a squeak and a thread of blood trickles down its nose. So little life that even the blood is pale.

The tomcat comes along, turns the dead mouse on its back and again on its belly until it stops moving. Bored, the cat bites off its head. It crunches between his teeth. Sometimes you can see his teeth while he is chewing. He leaves whining. The mouse's belly is still lying there, gray and soft like sleep.

He is full, Mother says. This is the fourth one I caught for him today. He doesn't catch any himself. They run between his paws and he sleeps, that lazy cat.

Baskets are filled with corn. The attic seems to get bigger and bigger. When it is totally empty it will be as big as it gets.

The corn cobs seem to roll into my hands and fall into the basket by themselves.

The palm of my hand hurts only when it's empty. While the corn rubs against it I stop feeling the pain, it is so strong, it is so overpowering that it kills itself. I feel a tingle, and then my hand and wrist and fingers are gone.

I take the cobs from the bottom. I make a tunnel for the flight of the mice. I have a big lump of fear in my throat, a thick lump of breath.

Two mice are climbing up the lattice wall. Mother strikes twice and they fall.

The cat bites off two heads. His teeth are crunching. It is October, and in October is the country fair.

The neighbor boy shot for me at a shooting gallery.

On metal sheets they had painted a chicken, a cat, a tiger, a dwarf, and a girl. The dwarf had a beard and looked like a Santa Claus.

The man at the shooting gallery had only one arm.

He took the money I held out for him standing on the tips of my toes. He loaded a gun with his hand and his knee. He gave the gun to my hunter.

My hunter was aiming. What shall I shoot, he asked. I looked at the metal sheets one by one.

The girl, I said, shoot the girl.

He shut his eye so tightly that his whole face got one-sided and looked as stern as the face of a real hunter.

He pulled the trigger, and the sheet tipped over. It was dangling for a while, then it came to a stop. The girl was hanging head down. She was doing a headstand.

Strike, the man at the shooting gallery said. Pick out something nice for yourself.

There were sunglasses, necklaces, dolls in stiff foam dresses, and wallets with pictures of naked women on the cover, all hanging from a string.

On the table top there were tumbler men and mice. One mouse looked especially podgy. I took it.

It was dark gray, had a square head, ears of rags, a leather tail, and a bobbin under its belly, with a long white thread. A shiny metal ring was fastened to the end of the thread.

I put the mouse on the smooth palm of my hand and poked the tip of my finger through the ring. Then I removed my hand.

The mouse whizzed to the ground and made a big curve. I followed it with my eyes, full of suspense.

It was clicking.

After it had stopped I laughed in quick spurts.

Then I rewound the thread, put the mouse again on the palm of my hand and poked the tip of my finger through the ring. Then I pulled my hand away.

The mouse whizzed to the ground and made a big curve, it was clicking again, and I laughed again.

I laughed till late at night when the lights in the village came on. The music was playing. The couples joined the dance leader. The children were skipping along the road after the train. You couldn't see them in the whirled-up dust. I heard them shout. They were dancing in circles at the corners, around and around, and then they were skipping on.

I held my mouse in my hand and went home on the sidewalk. That night the mouse was lying on the windowsill next to my bed.

The night was freezing to death. In the barns bright cats' eyes were stirring the fire. Snow fell on stray dogs.

I heard the pig. It was moaning.

Its resistance was so little that the chains were superfluous.

I was lying in bed. I felt the knife at my throat.

It hurt, the cut went deeper and deeper, my flesh got hot, it began to boil in my throat.

The cut got much bigger than me, it grew above the whole bed, it burned under the blanket, it moaned its way into the room.

The torn intestines were rolling over the rug, they were steaming and smelling of half digested corn.

Over the bed, a stomach full of corn was hanging on a bowel that got thinner and thinner and was twitching.

When the bowel was about to tear off I turned on the light.

I wiped the sweat off my forehead with the back of my hand.

I got dressed. My hands were trembling as I buttoned my clothes. My sleeves and my pantlegs were like a bag. All my clothes were like a bag. The whole room was like a bag. I myself was like a bag.

I went outside into the yard, I saw the big corpse hanging on the rack. Right above the snow was a round bloody nose, like a box. A big white belly like that of a pregnant fish. A big chewing mammal.

Blood spots on the snow. Snow White had skin as white as snow and cheeks as red as blood. Snow spattered with blood, snow and blood beyond the seven mountains.

Children listen to that fairytale and touch their velvety smooth cheeks.

The cold eats away at the gables of the houses with its salt. In many places the inscriptions are crumbling off. Letters and numbers fall into the seasons that are sitting on the fences like bony woodpeckers, and they peck at the housework of the women who are always alone during the day and who get caught in the dark folds of their skirts. Silently they walk between their walls, and behind their backs, the doors lean against the rooms croaking.

At noon they break the silence by their calls for the chickens who with tousled feathers fly into the yard, lured by shiny yellow kernels of corn. They scatter their feathers and bring the wind in from the streets.

The children leave the school shouting. The big children shove snow down inside the collars of the little ones, and bang their bookbags on their backs, and tear their hats from their heads, and throw them into the mud, and stick their heads in the snow.

And when their heads are blue with cold and fear they cry in torment and run into the houses with twisted clothes. The muffled-up men who leave the pub with their moth-eaten fur hats walk by thoughtlessly talking to themselves. They have purple lips and eyelids and resemble the snowmen who emerge from the fog at street corners, with their big bellies with which they would be able to run around the village.

In the spring, when the sun licks their hard bellies into foam you can see the tips of grass under their bellies, and in the cellars they put down beams on which the men stalk over to the wine barrels like big marsh birds. And when the wine gurgles in their throats the water gurgles in their shoes too.

That water is yellow and hard, and in the laundry it feels gritty, not foamy, and the clothes turn gray and rough from it.

The gaunt women drift along the streets in their long shifts.

In their empty mornings, they go to the store in the creased yokes of their blouses and the bony boxes of their scarves that sit like peaks on their heads, and they buy yeast or a box of matches.

And the dough they knead blows up like a monster and crawls through the house, mad and drunk with yeast.

At breakfast, the old women slurp the skin off the milk and chew wet sweet bread and still have the night's ooze in their eyes. And at noon they chew the starch out of the round white noodles.

On winter afternoons they sit at the window and knit themselves into their stockings made of scratchy wool; the stockings get longer and longer and they are as long as winter itself, they have heels and toes and hair as if they could walk by themselves.

And their noses above the knitting needles are getting longer and longer and they have a greasy shine like boiled meat. Drops hang on them for a while and glisten, then they fall into the aprons and disappear.

Their wedding pictures are on the walls. They have heavy wreaths on their flat blouses and in their hair. They hold beautiful slim hands over their bellies and young sad faces. And in the pictures next to those, they have children holding their hands and round breasts under their blouses, and behind them is a wagon piled high with hay.

While they knit they grow wispy beards on their chins that get paler and paler and grayer and grayer, and sometimes a thread of it gets lost in the stockings.

Their mustaches are growing with age, hair sticks out from their noses and warts. They are hairy and don't have breasts any more. And when they are finished with aging they resemble the men and decide to die.

Outside, the snow is glistening. Next to the roads the dogs have pissed yellow spots into the snow and stripped the stiff remainders of shrubs.

On the outskirts of the village the houses get lower, so flat that it's not exactly clear where they end. The village crawls into the valley over the big warty pumpkins that lie forgotten in the field.

In the dark the children carry their eerie drunken pumpkin lights through the village.

The pulp is scraped out of the pumpkins. Two eyes, a triangular nose and a mouth are cut into the shell.

A candle is placed in the pumpkin shell. The flame shines through the holes that are the eyes, nose, and mouth.

The children are swaying the cut-off heads through the dark. They run into the houses crying.

The adults are walking by.

The women tighten their scarves around their shoulders and get their fingers stuck in the fringes. The men grab their faces with their heavy coat sleeves.

The landscape dissolves into dusk.

The windows of our houses shine like pumpkin lights.

The doctor lives far away. He has a bicycle without a light and ties a flashlight to his coat button. I don't know which is the doctor and which is the bicycle. The doctor is much too late. My father's puked out his liver. There in the bucket it stinks like rotten soil.

With very large eyes, my mother is hovering in front of him waving air in his face with a huge kitchen towel crying.

In the cavity of my father's head, the candle has duped itself into death.

Old kitchenware lies scattered at the outskirts of the village. Dented ruined pans without bottoms, rusted buckets, small stoves with broken plates and without legs, stove pipes with holes. Grass with bright yellow blossoms grows out of a washbasin without a bottom.

The worm eats the bitter flesh of the sloe plums and presses a colorless juice through their thin blue skin.

The inner leaves are about to suffocate. The twigs are pushing out of the ditch, they end in long sharp thorns and get twisted in their search for light.

In the valley there is a strong iron bridge that the train crosses to go into the same plains, into a different village that looks exactly like this village. Under the bridge, there is snow in the winter and shade in the summer. There is never water under it. The river doesn't bother with it, it goes past it. In the summer, sheep gather here on hot days.

The stinging nettle whips its moving shadows into the village. Its fire creeps into your hands leaving red swollen stings behind, its tongues licking blood and hurting in the blood vessels of your hands.

The ducks disappear in the warm mud of the pond. They reappear on the opposite shore white and dry as if they hadn't been anywhere.

They are fat and their wings are stunted, and their brains, with measly circulation, have long forgotten that they are birds.

The women use their wings to brush flour or bread crumbs off the tables.

Their beaks are dripping with mud that falls back into the pond and creates a far-reaching ripple in the water.

In the summer, the women pluck the white down off their bellies. For the whole summer they waddle through the grass frazzled and drag their wings behind them and shrug them as if they were shoulders and walk in the furrows of the worms, and quack them into their throats and chew up the long jumps of the frogs.

And when fall comes they are slaughtered.

The feathers are plucked at the base of the neck about the width of a thumb. The main vein becomes visible and turns more prominent and blue with fear. With her slippers, Grandmother steps on the wings. The head is held back, the knife penetrates the thickest vein, and the slash spreads wider and open. The blood squirts and drips, then it flows into the white bowl. It is hot, and it turns black and threatening in the open air.

Grandmother is standing on the wings with her slippers, bowed and absent-minded she gazes after a fly, she puts her free hand on her back and complains about backaches.

The blood has finished dripping.

Grandmother takes her feet off the wings. The empty body twitches in its webs. Death has come, the white feathers again belong to a bird. Now it will fly.

The summer is high up above.

It disappears in a bucket of boiling water. Grandmother pulls it out by its legs. The feathers are wet now and seem sparse. Grandmother has put a bird into the water and pulls out a flimsy wool stocking, with a head that refuses to close its eyes. She plucks the feathers from the pores of the yellow skin and throws them into the water. They sink to the bottom. Some are floating at the rim of the bucket, floating in a circle as if they were looking for something.

Grandmother cuts into its breast. She raises the lid. There is steam and a smell of warmth and half-digested frogs.

The green mold of the pond has settled in the thin transparent maw.

Tomorrow is Sunday, and when the bell rings at noon, a heart and a wing will lie on my plate.

Have a nice Sunday, bon appetit!

Behind the barns, snakes slither in the milk of the dandelions and in the hair of the thistles. Sometimes the leaves or stems move. There is no one. Not even the wind.

You look across. The spasm grows, it hooks its claws into your flesh, then they slip off the bones of your feet and fall off. You look at the ground, you see your bloody shoes walking far off and alone, and fear winds itself through the hovering white plumage of the faded dandelions. Every leaf, every stem is a snake. The vermin swarm in the clover, gather and ball up in your throat and belly.

At night the dream comes through the backyard into your bed.

Out there is the stack of straw, its stalks rotten from rain like mud. Long black snakes crawl over it and dig themselves into it. It's dry inside the straw and bright yellow like the grass blossoms. The snakes are cold and wet.

The yard disappears, the gardens disappear, the whole house fades into the straw. No longer can you see the windows, no hedge, no trees, no roof. With her dull broom, Mother goes out into the street. And just as she wants to begin sweeping, a snake crawls onto her broomstick. She throws down the broom and runs off into the street crying and screams for help. The windows remain shut, the roller blinds remain shut. There isn't a soul in the whole village.

I wake up, my hair is tousled and wet on the back of my neck and my forehead. Grandmother says that I screamed in my dream.

The snakes crawl back into the teeth of the dandelions.

And then one day Grandmother brings back the snakes. They crawl from under the yoke of her blouse, from her vocal cords, from a conversation that always begins with "in the old days."

She kneads the salt into the dough where her arms have disappeared up to her elbows. I pour in more water.

Grandmother, you have such tough hands.

There used to be many snakes in the village. They would crawl from the forest through the river into the fields, from the fields into the gardens, from the gardens into the yards, from the yards into the houses. During the days they would slither behind the attic stairs, and at night they would suck up the cool milk from the buckets.

The women would take the children along to work in the yard and garden. They would put them in wicker baskets with blankets and put the baskets in the shade of the trees. From the beds they dug out clumps of grass with their roots and clods of soil. They would breathe, dig, and sweat.

She lived at the outskirts of the village. She was in the garden and had put her child in a wicker basket under the tree. A bottle of milk was lying next to the basket. She hoed in the potato foliage, looked up at the sun, smelled of sweat, put down the hoe and went over to the tree.

Her eyes went blank, her clothes stuck to her skin. She stiffened. She grabbed the child, she sobbed and screamed, and while she was staggering in the grass the snake slithered, long and lazy, from the basket into the grass, and in a few seconds the hair on the woman's head turned gray.

The hoe was left in the garden and the wicker basket under the tree. The snake had sucked the bottle dry.

The woman's hair remained gray, and so the people in the village finally had proof that she was a witch.

Witchcraft is all they talked about and they left her alone. They stayed out of her way and called her names because she did her hair differently, because she tied her scarf differently, because she painted her house differently than the village people, because she wore different clothes and had different holidays, because she never swept the street and on butchering day she drank as much as a man and was drunk at night; and instead of washing the dishes and salting the bacon she would dance alone with her broom.

And in the spring, after her husband had gotten pale and translucent, one morning he was lying stiff and cold in his bed.

She had to bury him in the reeds behind the cemetery where the water gurgled under your feet.

That summer the reeds grew higher and denser than ever.

The frogs croaked and got colder and swelled up bigger, the dragonflies were more snappy in their flight, trembling and getting stuck in the white dust of the snake flowers. They were dead and sat beautiful and empty in the reeds.

At night smoke rose from the reeds. The witch had been burning candles again.

That summer the village smelled more bitter than ever before. The weeds grew wild and furious and burned in lavish colors.

The women would whisper when they met each other in the street, and they pulled their scarves deep down over their faces, and they began to resemble each other.

Their voices turned as husky as those of the men from all that whispering, and their faces became hard.

Crowded together on creaking wagons, the men would go out to the fields and work silently. They would pull their scythes through the grass and sweat from work and silence.

There was no laughter or singing at the inn. On the walls, the flies would hum their mad insistent tunes.

The men would sit behind their tables, separate and sunk low, and pour that burning drink deep into their throats, then drop their short eyelashes, close their lips tight, and shift their cheekbones back and forth.

The gardens smelled humid and bitter.

The lettuce grew dark red and tough and would rustle like paper along the garden paths. And the potatoes were green and bitter under their skins and had eyes sunk deep into their flesh. They were small and hard and stayed in the soil during the winter. Their foliage, however, was high and lush spreading its blossoms into the summer.

The horseradish grew like foam in the beds, and its roots were hotter and woodier than ever. The rosehips remained green and sour. The summer was too wet for them.

The witch was standing at a street corner.

The women tore their white sheets into bows and tied them in the gardens. Above the bows the sky was black with scarecrows. All the gardens were full of them.

The women stuffed their husbands' suits with straw and pinned them up on high stakes. They put hats on their heads, the hats would swing in the wind, they didn't have heads or faces.

The birds were emaciated and hovered in the air screeching. Hunger was fluttering around. It grew in the forest and avoided the village which resembled a black island.

And when winter came the gardens turned bare. The garden beds were hard and empty. The scarecrows remained on their stakes and when it snowed grew into space as a warning. They turned into big magicians of ice and porcelain and stuck out high above the trees.

The snow fell into the village from their hats, the clouds clustered at their shoulders. The crows fluttered into the valley from their throats.

It would snow into the long hallway that was just one staircase above the street. In the yard the dead grass broke. The hens would squat together in the doorways. The branches were scattered all over the house. There was crackling in the house as in the forest. In the middle of the room there was a chopping block, next to it was an axe.

The sound of the axe is in the well. The witch is chopping her wood indoors again. There is a smell of burnt apples from her chimney.

Santas are walking around in the village.

The children are afraid of their nuts and oranges.

Merry Christmas.

For New Year's a letter arrives in the village. The mailman looks at the stamp for a long time. It's from an unknown place somewhere in the country. The name Lena doesn't exist in our village. The letter can only be for that colonist, for that young witch with the gray hair.

Sometimes Grandfather knows that he doesn't know what he knows. Then he walks through the house and the yard alone and talks to himself. Once when he was chopping turnips in the barn I saw him and he didn't see me. He was talking to himself, moving his arms without putting the axe down. He was chopping around in the air, then got up and walked around the basket of turnips and his face got more and more distorted. And for a moment he looked younger than he had in a long time.

Grandfather is plucking at his thick mustache. There are some whiskers that get stuck on his hand. He looks at them, throws them to the ground and never forgets to step on them.

For some nights now, Grandfather has been sleeping in the barn on the cartload container. The cow is supposed to calve. She stands with her behind right next to him and splashes that green runny turnip excrement on the straw, it spatters against the walls, sticks to the whitewashed walls like flies and evaporates in the air. The cow forgets to calve in this warm air.

The date on the Catholic calendar on the kitchen wall is long gone. Next to a circled date it says: cow covered. And next to other dates it says: started setting hen, delivered tobacco, bought pigs.

I look at the cow's big hard belly and doubt that she will stay alive with that belly. I think there's nothing but a big rock inside.

Even now I am not allowed to be there when the cow calves. I just always see the finished calf on the straw. It is rickety and its legs are trembling. They've sprinkled it with bran, and the cow licks the slippery integument from its skin.

Again I am angry at the trickery of sprinkling the calf with bran. I know that too is fraud.

The cat shows me her torn ear, and the snow is spattered with blood. Even when it's summer the stain remains, it always remains because I've seen it in this place.

My doll is sleeping with closed eyes, its face lying in the upholstery of the chair. I put it on its back. Its nose has been knocked off. It is wearing heavy winter clothes. Its eyes are ruined. I look into them, they are deep holes with plastic balls inside hanging on a spring. That's the way my doll's beautiful blue eyes are.

Frost flowers spin their tangles across the windows. I feel a beautiful shiver on my skin. Mother cuts my nails so short that my finger tips are hurting. With those newly cut fingernails, I feel I can't walk well.

I constantly walk on my hands. I also feel that I can't really talk or think well with these short nails. And the day is nothing but a huge exertion.

The frost flowers devour their own leaves, they have faces like milky blind eyes.

On the table the hot noodle soup is steaming. Mother says: let's eat, and if I am not there after the first call, if I am not standing close to the edge of the table, the traces of her hard hand are on my cheek.

Grandfather has to be called several times. Sometimes I think he does it for my sake. I like him when he doesn't listen to Mother.

He washes the sawdust off his hands and sits down in his place at the head of the table.

No one speaks another word. My throat is dry. I can't ask for water because I am not allowed to speak during dinner.

When I grow up I'll cook frost flowers, I'll speak during meals, and I'll drink water after every bite.

Father would come in and have those transparent shiny splinters on his boots. He would take off his gloves and sit down on a chair.

There was a puddle of cold quivering water on the floor where he had been standing, and he left wet boot prints on the wooden floor where he walked.

Then Father would take off his boots. They were tight and made of cowhide as hard as bone.

Father pulled his foot rags out of the bootlegs. They were wet with melted snow and sweat, and they were crumpled from walking.

Father's foot had a sole, and even in the winter that sole had a rough cracked heel. And in the evening when Father would smooth down those rough cracked heels with a roof tile they didn't get smoother or softer. They were part of him, as rough and hard as they were. And I don't think there was anyone in the village who didn't have these rough cracked heels. Perhaps it was the land where the village was located, which everyone called fields, that was the reason for these heels. The land was sticky and intractable. Mother hung the footrags on the rod of the kitchen range. They were made of striped material from one of the Sunday dresses I had grown out of. I had gotten the dress for Easter and had been very proud of it.

The photographer was in the village at the time. I was plump and had dimples on my wrists. My hair was made into a roll that was moistened with sugar water and twisted over the handle of a cooking spoon on holidays. It turned out crooked as it always did on holidays because Mother cried while doing my hair because Father had come home drunk from the pub again.

The holiday was spoiled as all holidays in this house are.

You can tell from this picture, from the crooked roll made of hair and sugar water and my crooked smile.

All combed and dressed I went to the backyard and locked myself in the outhouse, and I pulled down my pants, sat down over the smelly hole and cried loudly. I did my crying there so that I wouldn't be found out, and when I heard steps outside I quieted down quickly and rustled with the toilet paper because I knew that in this house you weren't allowed to cry without a reason. Sometimes Mother would beat me when I cried and say, see, now you have at least a reason.

I wiped myself with the toilet paper, and then looked into the hole and saw the feces with white worms crawling on them. I saw the little black balls and knew that Grandmother was constipated again, and I saw the light yellow feces of my father and the reddish feces of my mother. I was looking for my grandfather's feces when Mother shouted my name in the yard, and when I was finally standing in front of her in the room she stopped rolling the stocking up her leg and slapped me in the face, you have to answer when I call you.

And when we arrived at Grandmother's at the other end of the village Mother cried and said that Father comes home drunk every day. Father was sitting at the table and didn't touch the glass of wine that Grandmother had put in front of him, he got up, took his coat and left. Mother was leaning against the tiled stove with the palms of her hands and sobbed. I was nibbling on a piece of cake.

Mother was leaning her whole body against the tiled stove and crying in shrieks. Suddenly she realized that I was sitting on the stool watching her, and she screamed at me and Heini abruptly. Go outside, go play in the yard!

Heini and I stood in the yard not saying a word. Heini was chewing on his index finger.

I walked around the yard aimlessly, Heini disappeared between the corn stalks in the garden. I was standing next to the sandpile. There was a lot of shimmering stuff in the sand. The sand was dry although the sparkle in it seemed wet.

I began building a house.

Why do they call everything mothers do work and everything children do play? My house got cracks in the sun. I smoothed out the walls. Grandmother's house had wet rotten walls. Grandmother often whitewashed them, but the mildew ate right through the paint again. It was salty.

On summer evenings when the goats returned from the fields they would lick the walls. Inside there was a track of sand along the walls from the ants pushing in from the street.

There were also ants on the floor in the room. Grandmother had nothing against ants.

Once they had crawled into the sugar bowl. There were more ants than sugar crystals in it. They looked like poppy seeds and they were swarming around.

I was afraid of them, they were so small and so countless, and they didn't make any sound working. Grandmother picked out the individual sugar crystals and said that ants are neither dirty nor poisonous and that we could still use the sugar.

I didn't want to eat any of it and poured my tea into the bucket with drinking water when Grandmother left the kitchen.

During the day it was summer. When it got dark the seasons didn't make sense any more because you couldn't see them. Night was simply night. There was a thunderstorm outside. The rain was beating down on the roof. The water rushed from the gutters.

Grandmother hung a big sack over herself and dragged the big wooden barrel under the gutter. She wanted to catch rain water.

Rain water—I couldn't help thinking of velvet. It was soft, and my hair turned silky and soft from it.

Night had fallen. I never understood how this quiet nightfall happened. Every night the summer drowned carelessly in the middle of the village. Everywhere it would get pitch black and dead silent.

There was still some thunder and lightning. The blankets were lying on me like heavy snow. I had a lot of wet grass in my throat.

The room got bright from time to time. The big empty boxes that Grandmother had been keeping for years would rustle. On the ceiling, multipede ghostlike animals made of specks of light and shade moved around. The telephone wires would whip against each other and throw the streets here and there.

At night outside the trees were lashing at each other. I saw them through the walls. Grandmother's house had become like a house of glass.

The trees were slender, and yet they didn't break. They came closer and closer to my bed and gave off a lot of cold.

And I wanted to drink them because they were so colorless and cold, but they cut my face and said, we're not water, we're glass. Even the rain is made of glass.

Then the room got empty. Thunder was tugging at the roller blinds.

I heard Heini's urine splash into the piss pot, and I knew that I wasn't lying in this room alone.

I called Heini's name, and pissing he asked, are you afraid?

A little. Lightning brightened the room.

I saw Heini holding the piss pot in his hand, standing there with bent knees. And he was holding his penis with the other hand. It was very white in the light of the lightning.

I had to piss too. I got up and sat down on the pot, and I sucked in my belly to prevent the urine from making a sound. But it got louder and louder underneath, I didn't have the strength to let it just dribble.

Lukewarm it was running out of me. It was rushing.

Heini called me to come to his bed. I am not afraid of lightning, he said. I crawled next to him under the blanket and looked into the room. One of those animals of light specks was hanging on the closet door.

I looked at it.

I could like you if you didn't piss so strangely, from that extension. It is so ugly.

Don't worry, we'll cut it off tomorrow.

I am afraid I will have a child by you. I don't think you are supposed to do that, we pissed into the same pot.

Don't worry, then we'll just get married.

But you are my cousin.

Grandmother pisses a lot. She has a very low belly.

How do you know that?

But you can see that through her skirts.

And then the day let the summer's noises trickle through the walls. In the street was the village.

I went home between the necks of the geese. They were hissing after me, and I was afraid and I hurried. Often I would run outright.

The dog barked at me as if I were a stranger. Mother was at work. Father was at work. Grandfather was at work.

Grandmother was at home.

Grandmother was my mother's mother. The village was full of grandmothers.

I had to peel potatoes. The knife slipped into my finger. The starch burned in the wound. There was blood on the peeled potato. I dropped the potato in the water. I took it from the water and cut it into pieces. I didn't know where to cut it. There are so many decisions when you cut up a small potato. How long and how thick does a well-cut slice of potato have to be? Probably not a single one was cut properly. No one knew.

The last slice was crooked and ugly. I put it in my mouth and bit it into pieces, then spit it onto the potato peels. Bitten into such small pieces, it looked like puke. I put long serpentine potato peels on top to hide it.

Grandmother would sprinkle flour on the dough and knead it lengthwise and crosswise. And then she would cut off a corner and brush egg white on it. Grandmother's skirts would bob. Her apron was full of flour.

My other grandmother has big breasts, but this one is quite flat. And the other grandmother has a low belly. Heini saw it. Probably all grandmothers have a low belly. But with this grandmother you can't see it through her skirts.

Who knows, maybe Heini would see it. But he has just one grandmother, and I have two. Heini has it easy. Heini knows everything.

The bells are ringing for early Mass. Flocks of sparrows are fluttering up from the church tower and flying into the poplar trees. The branches are whipping against each other. They always move and carry the wind into the village, in wide cold circles so that the men have to hold onto their hats with one hand. The leaves that fall from the poplars are green and as healthy as the summer. The mayor says that the falling of the leaves in the middle of the summer is caused by the big bell which has been out of tune for years because of the rust that has collected on it. And the priest thinks it's caused by the fact that the little bell hangs too low in the belltower. So there are constant disagreements between the priest and the mayor of the village.

The women go around the corner. They pass the crucifix and cross themselves three times, first they touch their fingers to their foreheads, then their mouths, and then their chests.

Then they go up the four steps and lift their skirts at their hips so as to not step on the hem. At the hem the skirts are the heaviest, the widest, and the most beautiful.

Then there is a heavy wooden door and thick walls without windows except the small stained glass windows all the way up at the top. Those colors don't exist anywhere else, neither in the church nor in the street. The Mass is not allowed into the street, and the street is not allowed into the church. There is a creaking noise, and soon the heavy wooden door is closed again, and organ music is floating through space and buzzing around our heads like bees, until our ears have gotten used to it and our temples are no longer pounding with the music, until our eyes are no longer burning in the milk of the candles.

The women hastily dip the tips of their thumbs into the sandy holy-water font and make the sign of the cross on their foreheads, their mouths, and their chests, then they walk, gently and rocking as if they didn't want to feel themselves, to a pew where there is still a space left among all the skirts. Next to the pew they genuflect and spread their skirts on the floorboards, then they rise and sit down on the open seat, and again make the sign of the cross, and while making the sign of the third cross on their chests they find their way right into the middle of the prayer.

The organ is buzzing up there in the gallery. The organist has gummy blue eyes that get smaller and smaller and recede further and further into his head. He has very white hair and rigid frozen tufts of grass above his mouth and around his eyes. When he talks his dentures clatter. They would fall to the ground when he laughs if he didn't hold his hand under his chin even before he starts laughing. Any time he laughs too long and keeps his mouth too wide open his dentures drop into his hands.

Looking confused he pushes them back into his mouth, but then he stops laughing. He can never laugh to the end. And sometimes he says that growing old is ugly.

A year ago his dentures were too small. They were rubbing his gums sore. With those sore gums he went to the village dentist who opened the window wide and threw the dentures way out into the church gardens. The organist walked right into the clover. It had just been mowed and you could see the dentures from a distance. For a while they seemed as strange to him as the teeth of a dog. He picked them up and wiped the clods of soil sticking to them into his handkerchief. The dentist was still standing in the window frame and reached out his hand for them and he had wrinkles on his face out of fear. He moved his fingers as if he was waving. The organist put the dentures in his large white hand, and when he was back in the room the dentist was already filing white powder off the inside of the dentures and was almost going to be friendly. But the organist silently stared at the tongs and scissors lying on white cloth. When the dentist wanted to push the dentures in his mouth he closed his lips tightly and reached out his hand. Dentures in hand he walked out the door without saying good-bye.

Outside he put the dentures in his coat pocket, and outside the gate of the house he put them in his mouth. Now they were loose. They were too big. But the organist hasn't gone to the dentist since.

When he plays he pedals with his feet, holding his hat in one hand while he supports himself on the organ case with his other hand. He treads the pedal board at regular appropriate intervals as if he were bicycling, as if he were trying to get the organ case rolling. And the boards and the whole church begin to buzz under his feet.

While pedaling he closes his eyes and is absorbed in thought that sometimes tears like worn strings because he falls asleep while pedaling. But even in his sleep he treads the board at regular intervals.

While he is pedaling his pant buttons are always open. The organist closes them after each song, and if he forgets he doesn't do it until after Mass, and if he forgets even then he doesn't do it until he gets home where his wife, walking among bowls and pans, shouts the word shame throughout the house. As on every Sunday, she's oversalted the soup again and forgotten the cake in the oven.

Grandmother sits in the fifth row with me. Next to me is tall Leni. She is the tallest woman in the village. Out in the street she isn't as tall. But here she just sits motionless and with a face hard as stone. She looks as stiff as a stick. Her clothes are clean and ironed. Her frock and her blouse have many rows of velvet cord sewn on them. In her apron she has holes embroidered with black silk that shines even when not a single fleck of sun hits it. Tall Leni has very long and very straight fingers and her shoulders are as straight as those of a clothes hanger. She is beautiful but she looks very unapproachable and cold. I move away from her, close to Grandmother's apron. Grandmother looks at me angrily.

I drop my head back onto my neck. In church even heaven* is a wall. It is sky blue and covered with stars.

I ask Grandmother which is the evening star and she hisses stupid and continues praying. And then I think that the virgin Mary isn't really Mary, but a woman made of plaster, and that the angel isn't a real angel, and the sheep aren't real sheep, and that the blood is just oil paint.

Tall Leni prays into my ears, she is the real Leni. I look at Grandmother, not her face, but her hands.

All her sinews are tense, there is no flesh on them, just bones and parched skin. At any moment they could grow stiff in death, but they are still moving in prayer, and the rosary is rattling.

The rosary presses itself into Grandmother's knuckles and makes bruises on those small knotty hands that look like work itself, as scraped as the hard wood that is standing around the house everywhere, as scratched, as arabesque and old-fashioned as her furniture. On the benches there are long thick cushions reaching from one end to the other looking like swimming belts.

The priest acquired these cushions so that the village people would come to church in the winter too.

Even in the summer I am cold when I sit in these pews. It is always dark in here and the shivers that overcome me rise from the tiles. They are frightening like a large sheet of ice after you have walked too far on it already and you have no legs left and you have to continue walking on your face.

The walls, the pews, the Sunday clothes, the murmuring

*The German word "Himmel" means both sky and heaven.

women lunge at me and I cannot defend myself against them even by praying, not even against myself. My lips grow cold.

Wendel has come to church with his grandmother. I had to hold his hand from home to the door of the church. I had to walk with him through the whole village, along the empty village street, in the street where you can even see the bug that crawls across your path. Wendel gets to sit up on the gallery next to the organist and watches his roughshod foot.

Every Sunday when we leave church Wendel tells me that he wants to be an organist too. You pedal the board and can follow your thoughts, you pedal, and the others, all the others start singing, and when you stop pedaling they stop singing. Once Wendel was sitting in the children's pew in the front. He joined in the spoken prayers and confused the children next to him with his stuttering.

The priest threw a piece of chalk down from the pulpit. Wendel got a line of chalk on his coat collar. He stopped speaking and sat there motionless because you couldn't even cry during Mass unless you cried during or after the sermon.

You were also not allowed to get up.

Ever since that time, Wendel has walked up the narrow winding stairs to the organ gallery as soon as he has closed the door behind him.

He sits in an empty pew next to the organist.

The hunchback Lorenz sits on the other side in another empty pew.

Even during Mass, Lorenz is seized by this rough dry cough. The women in the choir turn their heads toward him while singing and make angry faces. Lorenz looks at their gullets moving up and down while they sing. He sees how the veins swell up on their throats and recede again into the skin. Kathi has a red hickey again on her throat, it moves along when she sings.

Lorenz averts his eyes, he looks at the armrest under his elbows. There are names and years scratched into it, also hearts and bows and arrows. Lorenz has scratched some of them in himself.

Lorenz used a long nail to scratch his own name into the wood.

Lorenz wrote his name on the organ case and you can see it from a distance. Lorenz likes to draw big letters.

On the central pillar it says: *Lorenz + Kathi*. Lorenz himself wrote it. On the dusty wall of the organ case it says *Lorenz* too, and the word stays there until a choir singer leans her back against it.

When the singing is over the murmuring of prayers starts down there in the pews. All the women kneel down, cross themselves with that threefold cross, murmur God-I-am-not-worthy, cross themselves again and rise.

I pray. Grandmother kicks me in my leg with her knee, I pray more softly. I want to pray myself free from all guilt. I know that Father had broken the calf's leg.

In the village you are not allowed to butcher calves or distill schnapps. In the summer, the whole village smells of schnapps, like a huge kettle of schnapps. They all distill their own schnapps somewhere in the yard behind the fence, and they don't talk about it, not even with their neighbors.

In the morning Father broke the leg of the calf with the handle of a hoe. Then he went to get the vet.

Around noon the vet rode his bicycle into the yard. He put it by the plum tree and when he had disappeared behind the barn door the chickens flew onto it.

In Romanian, Father explained to the vet how the calf got its foot caught in the chain on the manger and how it couldn't find its way out again, and how it fell over the pole with its whole body and broke its leg.

While he was explaining Father was stroking the calf's back. I looked into Father's face. You couldn't tell that he wasn't telling the truth. I wanted to push his hand from the calf's back, I wanted to throw his hand into the yard and crush it. I wished his teeth would fall out for this lie.

Father was a liar. All of those standing around were lying because of their silence. All of them were staring into space. I looked at them one by one, those ugly grimy faces, those noses, those eyes, those shaggy hairy heads. Father's whiskers had doubled and were hiding his brutality. Father's hands were groping for words that were lies and everything they did they did with conviction.

Then the vet was rustling a notebook out of his grimy bag. He wrote something on a piece of paper, tore it out and held it in front of Father's face. Even while the vet was still writing, Father had put a one-hundred-lei bill into his pocket, and the vet pretended that he didn't notice anything and continued writing.

Then he held the paper in his hand, it said that the calf had had an accident. It was a permit for an emergency slaughter.

The vet also finished the eighth glass of schnapps in one gulp, then he shooed the chickens off his bicycle. They flew off in all directions and cackled in the air. On his seat there was a heap of fresh chicken shit. I was happy because when he wiped it it spread all over the seat. The bicycle rolled out the gate, the vet threw himself on it sideways and rode off with his back hunched over. His butt was hanging off the seat on both sides, like Grandmother's dough swells over the edges when she bakes bread. The bicycle was creaking under his weight. Uncle brought a big hammer from the backyard.

Mother tied the apron on him. He had a big bow squirming on his butt. Then she rolled up his sleeves to his elbows and didn't want to stop rolling them up. Mother seemed very flirtatious because she laughed so much while she was doing it.

Mother rolled up Father's sleeves too, she did it very fast and was not flirtatious. Mother rolled up her own sleeves too and did it fast not showing any expression in her face.

Grandfather pulled his arm away and rolled up his own sleeves.

I was afraid. They all had hair on their arms. I pulled the sleeves of my blouse over my hands and with my fingers held them shut from the inside like a tied-up sack. I had to stand there for a while with tied-up sleeves in order not to turn violent, not to scratch or choke someone.

The swallow next to the beam was leaning forward with its whole white belly over the edge of its nest looking toward us. It didn't make a sound. When Uncle lifted his heavy hammer I ran into the yard, stood under the plum tree and held both hands over my ears. The air was hot and empty. The swallow didn't come with me, it had to brood over an execution.

A village full of strange dogs was in our yard. They were licking the blood from the straw of the manure heap and dragging claws and skin scraps across the barn floor. Uncle pulled them from their mouths. They weren't allowed in the street with them.

Two eyes were lying in the liquid manure. The cat bit into one of them with her canine tooth. There was a crack, and bluish slime splattered in her face. She shook herself and walked off with stiff spread-out legs.

Uncle sawed a bone that was as thick as his arm.

Father nailed the large red-speckled skin to the wall of the barn to dry. The midday sun fell on it. After a few weeks I had a calfskin in front of my bed.

Every night I carried the bedside rug outside because at night I would feel all its hair in my throat. I dreamed that I had to eat the skin with knife and fork; that I ate and vomited and had to go on eating and vomited more hair, and Uncle said, you have to eat everything or you will die. When I was dying I woke up.

The next night Father forced me to ride the calf. He chased us across a field. The flowers grew high and dense. When we were in the middle of the field the calf's back broke under me. I wanted to get off. But Father screamed and chased me through all the fields around us, and there were so many that there was just no end to them. Father chased us through the river, Father was howling and we were riding through the forest following our echo.

The calf was panting and, and in a panic, rammed its head into a tree. Blood was running from its nostrils. Blood was on my toes, on my beautiful summer shoes, on my dress. When the calf collapsed the ground beneath me was full of blood.

Mother turned on the light and said good morning and put the red-speckled calfskin in front of my bed. When I got up the room was turning, there was a lot of hot sun on my face, and I took a big step over the calfskin rug. At noon Mother brought her milking pail from the barn into the kitchen. There was foam on the milk. I was looking for pink milk in the pail. There just had to be blood in it. The pail was warm. I put my hands around it and clasped it tight for a long time.

For days the cow was mooing into the empty straw. She didn't touch her food. For days she would just slurp water, just cold water, and while drinking she immersed her head in the pail up to the tips of her ears.

Every day at noon, Mother brought warm milk to the kitchen, warm from the cow. I asked her if she would be sad too if they took me away from her, if they were to slaughter me. I fell against the closet door, I had a blue bump on my forehead, I had a swollen upper lip and a purple bruise on my arm. All that from a slap.

Mother said, now that's enough crying. I had to stop sobbing that second and speak friendly to my mother the next moment. Children are not supposed to hold grudges against their parents because everything the parents do the children have coming to them. I had to admit loudly and voluntarily that I had that slap coming to me and that it was too bad for every missed slap. Grandmother brought in the big broom. A bowl had fallen out of the closet when I fell against it.

Grandmother began sweeping.

Mother grabbed the broom from her hand and posted it in front of me. I swept up the broken pieces and with all those tears I saw the kitchen only in a blur.

The broom handle was taller than I was. It moved back and forth in front of my eyes. The broom handle swirled around, the kitchen swirled around.

Mother made a very wrinkled face. Move.

On the pavement, mothers walk in Swabian skirts sewn of whole bales of material; while walking, their creases resemble treetops that sprawl on the roofs of houses and push the village into the grass and beat the roofs when it is windy and break roof tiles. The mothers carry white ironed handkerchiefs stuck under their apron strings. This morning they crept out of their beds in order to cry, they had breakfast and lunch in order to cry.

They bundle every household job into chores and movements, and their heads are bowed in the search of absence and the flight from themselves. A whole day long they come out of their shells into the wood and cloth and tin of their households.

And at noon they loosen the cords on their aprons and frocks, drop them to the floor and take their black dresses from their closets.

And when they approach the closets they look up to the ceiling so that they won't see themselves naked because in every room of the house anything can happen that you would call shameful or impure. You just have to look at yourself naked in the mirror or realize that you are touching your skin when you roll up your stockings. Dressed in clothes you are a human being, and without clothes you are not. That whole large area of skin.

They dress in order to cry, black from their shoes to the fringes of their scraggy scarves, and bob their creases back and forth.

It only appears that their daughters have abandoned their regional costumes. In their movements, the cloth bales of their Swabian dresses unfurl, and despite their skinny bodies they seem as if they don't fit into their clothes, as if they were outside their seams. But their brains are dressed in them.

In their tight clothes and with bare legs they trip along in silent dependence next to the bobbing shady frocks. They too wear black shoes and black dresses, but their black stockings are transparent.

In their hands they hold big black triangular patent leather purses that stiffly sway back and forth and look as though they are made of tin. Their sides are pushed in because they never contain more than a handkerchief and a rosary and the jingle of small change at the bottom.

And they don't know how to hold these purses because carrying these purses is totally different from grasping the handles of brooms, hoes, or kitchen knives, or the action of physically punishing their pets and children. For a few steps they carry them in their hands, then let them slide down to the bend of their arms where they hang like on pointed hooks and hit their flat butts when they walk; then they take them in their hands again and rub their thighs with them when they walk.

Despite the oppressive heat the daughters are wearing black scarves because their hair is either blond or black, but even when it's black it's not black enough for crying.

Like swarms of black birds they sweep into the house where the night guard lives, trample down the yard with their silent deliberate siege, walk by the open door of the summer kitchen and see what's left of the rope hanging from a beam.

Their big fish-cold eyes open wide, and they bring their chill into the candle-lit room filled with plastic flowers and the smell of a corpse. The devil stands paralyzed behind the door in the mirror which is covered with black Swabian aprons so that the prayers of the living and the soul of the dead man will go to heaven. The mothers and daughters dribble holy water from a sprig of evergreen on the coffin, and the water seeps through the veil and trickles down the cheekbones of the dead body onto the bruised throat, and the face turns yellowish-green and fat.

And while they are dribbling their eyes search for a chair. While they sit down the mothers are tucking at their skirt creases and the daughters arrange their angular purses on their thighs; and sniffling, the mothers wrap their rosaries that rattle like harnesses around the blue joints of their hands, and the daughters dab their eyes with handkerchiefs and force tears onto their faces. The men stay in the yard and pace up and down. And in front of the summer kitchen among swarms of flies above their heads, they talk about their work in the field and the wine in their cellars.

Behind the wire fence in the backyard there are still traces of chicken and the summer kitchen nights with their mad tracks in the sand. Floating in the air there are still glances tousled by chills like straw stacks, by a fever in the lungs eaten by cancer, and by the face of death; that face descends from the apricot tree ever silent and limber like a cat. It always appears unexpected, silent and sneering, and it smells.

The flowers in the flower beds stir above the screeching balled-up cats who pump heat into their bellies, who moan when the semen spurts into their bellies and who have their teeth full of sand from their screams.

The chickens on the mulberry tree got scared out of their sleep, they flap in the air for a while and numbly fall to the ground, finally they ramble in concentric circles on the sand, in smaller and smaller circles until they are reduced to touching just one point and they get so heavy that their legs won't carry them any more.

Then they fall over and turn their necks, open their beaks, and drown in the dark. The moon falls and falls.

Chicken lice twitch in the pores of their skins; in straight lines they march through the gardens into other yards, into hot living flesh. The mothers and daughters come into the yard from the room. The men pair up and go ahead into the street. Arms linked, the women follow them in pairs.

The big wind instruments are gleaming in the sun.

The music shatters on the walls of the houses and at the end of the street it comes back over the village.

The black coachman on the black carved funeral coach whips his black horses. The horses' legs are covered with flies. They walk with their butts in the coachman's face and let their urine flow into the sand, and they are startled by the loud music and mix up their hooves in their confusion.

The priest rattles the censer past the church because some dead people cannot be taken into the church if they do not humbly wait until God takes their lives and grants them death, but instead take their own lives without fearing God. The priest clears his throat with satisfaction.

In the cemetery, a flock of black crows flies above the big white marble crucifix that rises above the cemetery, and the sparrows whiz into the field out of the blackthorn along the road.

In front of the grave, the priest lets a big white monster of incense fly into the air and he sings. The priest throws the first big clod on the coffin and as if following a signal each of the black birds picks up a clod and drops it on the lid; they have big eyes and make the sign of the cross. The grave diggers stick the schnapps bottles into their coat pockets, spit into their hands, take the shovels and build a wet mound. The swarms of black birds disperse over the village and slip into the crevices of the fences and houses. The streets are finally empty. The sun sets in the cornfield and it has a red misty face.

When it rained Grandmother would look into the little bubbles that hit the pavement, and then she knew how long the rain would last.

She could tell when it was going to rain by looking at the cows and the horses and the flies and the ants. We have rain wind today, she said, and the next day it would rain. Grandmother stretched out her hand into the rain and left it there until strands of rain would drip off her elbow. When her hands were wet she would walk all the way out into the rain.

When it rained she would look for some job in the yard and let herself get wet down to her skin. It was a rare day when she went without a scarf, when I could see her thick folded braid that collected a lot of water so it became so heavy that it would drop to her side. Her hair too would get wet down to the skin.

A smell of wild plants wafted into my face from the gardens. It tasted bitter to my gums and got sticky on my tongue when I breathed. The bushes dragged their leaves. Rain would drip down.

I wore a dress of humid air. I had found a pair of big shoes next to the door. They belonged to Father; everything in this house belonged to someone, especially clothes and shoes and beds. Not a single night were beds or rooms exchanged, not a single lunch the places at the table, not a single morning did Father and Grandfather trade their clothes. It was just me who, when Mother was at work, sometimes walked through the house in beat-up felt slippers, in Father's oily shoes, in Grandmother's scarves that fill the house with the smell of naphtha.

A toad was jumping across the pavement. Its skin which was wrinkled and much too big formed creases all over. It crawled into the strawberries. Its skin was so awfully shriveled that not one leaf would rustle.

I felt cold on my heels and my calves.

The cold sprained my cheekbones. My teeth were cold. My eyeballs felt cold. The hair on my head hurt, I felt how deep into my head it had grown. And it was wet down to the skin or just cold, but that was the same thing. It was sharp, its tips were exposed to the night, it had cracked under its own weight and length.

I locked the night out into the yard. The door was warm and dry on the inside. The wood felt good to my hands. I touched it with my hand several times and was startled to realize that I was caressing a door. I put my feet next to each other and then stepped out of Father's shoes into the hallway, with my stockings on the bare wood, and my ankles went ahead of me to the kitchen. I opened the kitchen door still shivering for a while, and Mother asked if it was cold outside, if it was cold outside again. She stressed the word again, and I thought that it is cold outside, but not cold again because the cold is different every day, always a different cold, every day a new cold full of white frost. But it wasn't cold, it was just humid. You were afraid again, she said.

Mother and Father had eaten their supper.

Grandmother and Grandfather were already in their room. You could hear the radio through the wall.

On the table in the kitchen there were plates with sauerkraut and smoked sausages. There were pork rinds and bread crumbs on the table. Father had pushed his chair way back and was leaning against the wall. He was picking his teeth with a match.

It was in the evenings that I was allowed to comb Father's hair. Father had thick hair. I was able to sink my hands into it up to their roots. The threads of his hair were brittle and heavy. Sometimes one hair crept under my skin, then I went hot and cold.

I would look for the white hairs. I was allowed to pull them out, but they were very few. Sometimes I didn't find a single one.

I was allowed to part his hair, tie bows into it, and pull wire bobby pins over the skin of his head. I was allowed to tie scarves on his head and to drape scarves around his shoulders and hang necklaces around his neck.

But one thing I wasn't allowed to do was touch Father's face.

If I did it anyway, by mistake, Father would tear off all the bows and pins, the scarves and necklaces and push me away from him with his elbow and scream: Go away, now. I would always fall down and begin to cry and bite through the comb because of my hurt feelings, and at such moments I would know that I didn't have parents, that these two were nothing at all to me. And I asked myself why I was sitting there with them in this house, in this kitchen, why I knew their pots and their habits, why I didn't just run away, to a different village, to strangers, and why I wouldn't just remain a moment in each house, and then move on before the people turned bad.

Father didn't say a word. Once and for all I was made to understand that he couldn't stand hands in his face: That's my death.

I wished that a hand would grow from his nose or from his cheek, one he would always have on his face and he couldn't push away. Only when he washed his face were his hands on his face, but then they were his own hands, and it was more foam and soap on his face than hands. Father's anger made his cheekbones and his chin twitch.

He would have liked to play with you, said Mother, but you always have to spoil everything, now just stop crying.

I wanted to say something, but my mouth was so full of tongue that I couldn't get out a word.

I looked at my hands. They were lying on the window sill in front of me as if they had been chopped off, quite motionless. My nails were dirty again. I sniffed at my hand and couldn't figure out the smell. The dirt didn't have a smell, and my skin didn't have one either.

I moved my fingers as if they were very cold. They wanted to fall to the ground, but I remained in my chair bolt upright.

The red bow was lying next to the table leg. I picked it up and put it on the window sill. Right away I picked it up again and squashed it in my fist. When I opened my hands the skin inside was full of wrinkles and sweat, and the bow was crumpled and moist. I cleaned my nails with a wire pin and noticed how flat and wide they were.

Father was sitting behind his newspaper. He would crawl into the letters. Behind the wall, Grandfather's radio talked about Adenauer. Mother was sitting behind a white rag. Her needle went up and down between her forehead and her knees. As usual, Mother and Father talked very little, and the little was a lot about the cow and about money. During the day they would work and not see each other, and at night they would sleep back to back and not look at each other.

Mother was sewing a wall hanging. The one above the kitchen range had a lot of rust stains from the wire of the clothesline and had gotten thin. The woman who was standing at the kitchen range had only one eye. Her other eye and part of her nose had gotten caught in the washing machine. In her hands the woman was holding a bowl and a cooking spoon, and a flower was stuck in her hair.

What I liked is that she was wearing high-heeled shoes. Underneath her shoes you could read the saying: *Here's my advice, oh husband dear: forget the tavern, wine, and beer. Stay at home for supper too, and love your wife, or else we're through.*

Mother had a lot of wall hangings in the house. Over the table in the kitchen there was one with apples and pears, with a bottle of wine and a headless baked chicken. The line underneath: *Tasty Fare, Good-bye Care.*

Everybody in the house liked this saying. Mother had to write it on a scrap of newspaper for many people who came because they wanted to embroider it too.

Mother said that wall hangings were very beautiful and also taught you a lot. Mother would sew only at night when the house was clean and the yard was cold and so full of night that you couldn't go outside.

During the day, Mother had no time for sewing. And several times every day she said that she didn't have time, that she was never finished with all her work. Sewing wasn't work, so she sewed at night.

Mother never got a break from her drudgery. But the village people didn't praise her for her hard work. But they did talk about the neighbor woman, they said that she was no good, that she read books in broad daylight, that their whole household was topsy turvy and that her husband wasn't any better because he tolerated it all.

Mother's eyes are either in the bucket or on the floor.

Every Saturday Mother scrubs the hallway, she'll kneel for hours.

One day, I am sure, Mother will kneel in the middle of the sand pile and wash pathways through and through. And she will have all the sand under her nails. The sand will have dried again and come trickling together. One night Mother dreamed of that sand, and in the morning she told us the dream and she giggled, but its images showed on her sore skin.

The floor planks in the whole house had rotted from getting washed every day. The woodworm escaped from the moisture into doors, tabletops, and doorhandles. It gnawed mealy grooves even into the frames of the family pictures. Mother swept up the wood meal with a new broom.

She bought all her brooms from broom-maker Heinrich. Their sticks were rough and smudged with grease stains and sticky with burned sugar. The broom-maker's wife baked cake every day. One day she would make doughnuts, the next sugar pastry. The dough smelled of yeast even after the cake had been baked.

The house was full of yeast and spilled sugar. On the kitchen range there was a little pot of milk with dissolved yeast. On the edge the milk formed a big dim bubble that looked like an eye with a squint-eyed look.

The broom-maker's wife had seven cats in the house. They had no names, but they all knew who the others were, and so did the broom-maker and his wife.

The youngest slept in the egg basket and hadn't ever broken an egg.

The oldest slept under the table on its stand. Her belly would droop from the board on both sides. She would snore, and the broom-maker always said that it was because of her age. And when he was asked how old she was, he said very old and didn't look you in the face, and he would quickly look for some job that would make him bend down so that his head was down and his butt sticking up. His hands would lie on the floor under his knees.

The kittens that were born in the winter were drowned in a bucket of boiling water, and those born in the summer in a bucket of cold water. In the winter and in the summer, they were hastily buried in the middle of the manure pile after they were drowned.

During the night, there was a rustling noise from the garden, and the broom-maker got up and went out to the kitchen and paced up and down the rug.

The next day he took his sickle and cut the brushwood's legs off and tied them into bundles.

He would cut a little and drink a little. In the evening he stared into space a little and drank a little, and stared into space and drank a little, and drank a little, and was still out there after all the brushwood was lying on the ground in bundles. He always carried the schnapps bottle in his coat pocket. Even the sweat and urine he splattered in the garden smelled of schnapps.

His eyes would slide everywhere. Sometimes they would swim across his face. They were moist and dull and cold. The wind fumbled at the inside of his sweaty shirt.

The emptiness of the garden was like a large hollow. The broom-maker's shoes couldn't find their way out of this trough. His knees were knocking against each other when he walked. His feet got mixed up and wanted to walk on top of each other.

He saw many shoes ahead of him and had nothing to do with them, and again and again he stepped on them with shoes that he didn't have any more to do with. None of all those shoes were his shoes, and none of all those legs were his legs.

The cats are sleeping, purring, and eating in the house by now. When they come in from the yard they cross the threshold with their fur ruffled and their legs stiff. They bristle up their hair till their bodies recapture a little warmth.

In the evening they sit around the hind legs of the cow and watch the milking hands of the broom-maker's wife. They have knots in their bowels and bite their tongues impatiently.

They keep staring at those milking fingers. White milk is squirting from the udder. Their eyes become glassy and clear like grapes. The broom-maker's wife sticks the pail between her legs. She bites her lower lip. Her mouth is like a line, hard and thin. The vein at the root of her nose swells up, she presses her forehead against the cow's belly. The cow lowers her head into the crib and eats. Sometimes she swings her filthy tail in a small circle. Her legs stand stiffly in the straw.

The broom-maker's wife pushes the milking stool away from her. She lifts up the pail. She pours foaming milk from its spout into a big bowl. She cuts up a slice of bread and dips big pieces into the milk.

She puts the bowl on the floor. The cats jump over her arms and press around the bowl's edge. They are moaning with greed. Their tongues are getting long and red. The weaker cats are standing outside the circle. They watch from behind as if that could satisfy them.

On winter nights the cats go up the attic stairs to the attic. They carry their glowing eyes ahead of them. They hiss into the flour bins and walk around the smokehouse. They lean against the smoked sides of bacon and lick the salty edges. They have chitin and wasp shells hanging in their whiskers when they come back down. In their ears they have dirty ear-wax. They leave smudges of flour and soot on the wall where the brooms are.

The finished brooms were always placed against the wall of the hallway, sticks down. The cats walked between them and when a broom fell a cloud of dust rose from the tamped-down dirt, and the cat jumped over the garden gate in one leap.

Every month Mother bought one of those leaning brooms. Those brooms always smelled of doughnuts and plum schnapps, and they were always full of dust and little spiders.

After going through the gate out to the alley, Mother would take the broom she just bought directly to the water pump and pump a lot of water on it. The water was clear when it flowed into the broom and ran out dirty into the yard.

Mother beat the broom against the fence making all the pickets creak, and little shiny seeds sprayed from the brushwood onto the pavement and kept running over the stones for a while. When they stopped you couldn't see them any more. They were no longer shiny.

With her new broom Mother first sweeps the walls.

Mother has a living room broom, a kitchen broom, a front yard broom, a back yard broom, a cow barn broom, a pigpen broom and a henhouse broom, a woodshed broom, a barn broom, as well as a house floor broom, a smokehouse broom, and two street brooms, one for the pavement and the other for the grass.

Mother has a lot of summer brooms for the leaves that fall to the ground, she has many winter brooms for the snow that covers the yard and the street. All those brooms have long sticks. Mother also has many brooms with short handles. Mother has a brush for breadcrumbs in the table drawer, a carpet brush on the window sill, a linen brush between hers and Father's beds, a clothes brush in the closet, a dust brush on the closet.

With her brooms Mother keeps the whole house clean.

Mother sweeps the dust from the case of the wall clock. She opens its door and sweeps the dial too. With the smallest brush Mother sweeps the water jug, the candle sticks, the lampshade, the glasses cases, and the medicine boxes. Mother brushes the radio knobs, the prayer book cover, and the family pictures.

Mother sweeps the walls with her new long-handled broom.

She tears the webs off the spiders' bodies. The spiders flee underneath the furniture. Mother finds them even there, Mother lies down on her tummy and squashes them with her thumb.

Mother hangs up a new wall hanging. *The early bird catches the worm.* Above the proverb you can see a bird of green wool with a wide open beak. I have known that bird ever since I was able to see. I heard it much later. It only sings when no one is in the room. When anyone comes in it stops singing. But it keeps its beak wide open even when it's not singing.

But once it closed its beak. I ran fast to get Grandmother. But when I was standing in front of the bed with her its beak was wide open again. The bird was winking with one eye. But that's something I didn't tell Grandmother anymore because she was mad anyway since I had made a fool of her by getting her in from the backyard. With her rough hand she pulled my earlobe and shouted: I'll tear your ears off your head.

Mother lifts out the windows and washes them in a big tin tub. They are so clean that you can see the whole village in them, as if in the mirror of the water. They look like they were water. The village looks like it was water too. It makes you dizzy if you look at the village in the glass for a long time.

Everything is clean. Mother darkens the rooms and the hallways. The whole house is deserted and dark. Even the flies buzz bewildered through the last open door. Mother closes that door too. For a while she is standing there in the yard as if she were locked out. The glaring sun is blinding her for a while. Mother covers her eyes with her hands like a visor.

Mother hears chirping noises from the gutters. Sparrows have made a nest there. Mother learns how to see again. She goes to the backyard to get the long ladder.

The nest is small and loose. It is hanging on her broom and then falls to the ground. Cries in gray wrinkled skin drop to the pavement. The cat is sitting there on her hind legs with her tail lying quiet and straight behind her. The baby birds are still squeaking in her throat. They are still resisting in her gullet. Placidly the cat looks at the sun.

Mother is still standing on the long ladder. The rungs are flattening out the soles of her feet. The soles of my mother's feet are right above me. She squashes my face. Mother stands on my eyes and pushes them in. Mother stomps my pupils into the white of my eyes. Mother has dark blue mulberry stains on the soles of her feet.

Mother looks at me sideways. That half of her face is big and cold like a half moon. Mother has only this half of her face left, and in it her eye is as narrow as a slit. The ladder is wiggling, and Mother is wiggling over the village. With her hands, Mother can touch the dead sitting in heaven.

The air above the village is hot, there is not a bird in the air, it is late afternoon.

The gate to the street squeaks. Father comes in. Father is home early. Father can walk straight today, Father is not drunk.

My heart is beating with joy. I am anticipating the evening. There is fear too in that joy. My heart is beating with fear in that joy, with fear that I can't feel happy again, with fear that fear and joy are the same.

I tried to eat dinner. My teeth didn't fit together. The saliva in my mouth had a taste as if it wasn't mine. Even the water I wanted to drink got stuck in my throat.

Maybe tonight will be one of those few quiet nights. I might be allowed to comb my father's hair again, maybe I'll find a gray hair, then I'll pull it out by its root.

Maybe I'll tie a red bow into Father's hair. I won't touch his temple today.

Never again do I touch Father's face. That's his death.

Once Grandmother had fallen on the pavement around the well again. Her frock wasn't quite pushed up under her arms, and I laughed a lot. I also knew that she hadn't fallen so hard because of the pavement but because of my laughter.

So Grandmother got a cast on her arm. She had it for a whole summer. You could see her hand, a real hand, at the end of her cast. Grandmother's cast was very beautiful. It was snow white and looked very sturdy. Once I told Grandmother that it looked good on her. She got angry and threw her slipper at me. She didn't hit me, but I started to cry.

Grandmother's cast had gotten dirty with time. The city doctor who had given her this cast had a bloated and very pale face. When he saw Grandmother's cast his face got even bigger.

On her cast there were a few splashes of cow manure, some traces of green tomato leaves, many blue plum stains and some grease stains. There was a whole summer on her cast, and the doctor seemed to have something against that summer. He gave her a new cast. The first cast was more beautiful. I didn't like this new cast. It was snow-white, and Grandmother looked a little awkward with it.

Grandmother had taken me to town with her that day.

We went to a park with her new cast. There Grandmother fed me white bread and salami. Some pigeons were tripping back and forth in front of our bench. They were not afraid of me, and they picked up the bread I threw out for them.

Grandmother shook the bread crumbs from her apron, we got up, and I got a big pink ice cream while Grandmother, even before I began licking it, stressed that I didn't deserve the ice cream because I didn't obediently sit still in my seat on the train. I wanted to pick red poppies in the field, I wanted the train to stop. It wouldn't have taken me long at all. I would have picked the flowers quickly. But the train raced madly past all those red poppies.

Every time I went down to the valley with Grandfather to pick up sand, a train that was more beautiful than ever would pass by the river. I heard it from far away. It made beautiful rhythmic noises and there were heads in the windows. I jumped with joy and waved. And the hands in the windows waved back. Even when they were really far away they would still be waving.

Sometimes there were women in the windows who were wearing beautiful summer dresses. I could never see their faces very well, but I knew that they were as beautiful as their dresses and that these women would never get off at our station which was too small for them. They were too beautiful to get off at our station.

I didn't want to intimidate them with my waving, maybe they were shy. My hands got heavier and heavier from waving and dropped down.

There I stood next to the roaring train and looked into its wheels, and I had the feeling that the train came out of my throat and wasn't worried about tearing my bowels and that I would die. It is taking those beautiful women to the city, and I will die here next to a pile of horse dung where flies are buzzing around.

I looked for a patch of grass without gravel. I wanted to fall on my back so I wouldn't scratch my face. I wanted to cool down in the shade and be beautiful in death.

And I am sure they'll put a beautiful new dress on me when I am dead.

It was high noon, and death didn't come.

I imagined them asking themselves how I could have died so unexpectedly. And Mother would cry a lot for me, and the whole village would see how much she had loved me.

But death still didn't come.

From the tall grass, summer rolled its heavy scent of flowers over me. The wildflowers crept under my skin. I went to the river and poured water over my arms. Tall bushes grew out of my skin. I was a beautiful swampy landscape.

I lay down in the tall grass and made myself trickle into the earth. I waited for the big willows to come to me from across the river, to root their branches in me and spread their leaves in me. I hoped they would say: you are the most beautiful swamp in the world, we are all coming here. And we'll bring our tall slender water birds with us, but they'll flutter around in you and will scream in you. And you can't cry because swamps must be brave, and you must endure everything if you associate with us.

I wanted to expand so that the water birds with their wide wings would have room enough in me, room to fly. I wanted to nurture the most beautiful marsh marigolds because they are also heavy and bright.

Grandfather had already shoveled a pile of sand onto the river bank. I collected the shells that were broken open. I took them to the water and drank from them. They were white and shiny like enamel, and the water was yellow and full of yellow soil and tiny animals that looked like soil too, except they would wriggle.

There was sand between my teeth. I bit on it, and it crunched and scratched between my tongue and gums. Suddenly I realized how painful it must be when shellfish die.

There was sand in my pants. It rubbed me sore when I walked, and this was the same pain that shellfish felt when they died.

I walked into the water up to my belly. My pants got wet and bulging. The water was part of my belly. I slipped my hand behind the elastic waistband of my pants and washed off the sand between my legs.

While I was doing that I had the feeling that I was doing something forbidden, but no one saw me. Grandfather looked after his sand which kept falling onto the bank. But God is everywhere. This sentence that I kept hearing in religion classes occurred to me. I looked for God in the trees and so I found him with his big white beard high above the leaves, high up there in the summer.

Every time I sat in front in the children's pew, the Madonna had her finger raised. But she always had a friendly face at the same time, so I was not afraid of her. She also wore that light blue long dress and had beautiful red lips. And when the priest said that lipsticks are made from the blood of fleas and other disgusting animals I asked myself why the Madonna at the side altar was using lipstick. I also asked the priest and then he beat my hands sore with his ruler and sent me home immediately. I couldn't bend my fingers for several days afterward.

I went into the garden behind the straw stack and lay down in the clover and looked up at the sky. There wasn't a single cloud covering this hot day, and I couldn't find God's beard in the whole wide world. That day God was not everywhere.

Grandfather was still shoveling sand from the river. His floppy knee-length underpants were sticking to his legs. Between his thighs they looked like webs.

I saw a big bulge under the cloth. It was where Grandmother had a big bunch of hair. So that was the big secret the adults shared.

Grandfather had a lot of hair on his chest and legs, and on his arms and his hands. On his back he had two big hairy shoulder blades.

Grandfather's hair was wet and stuck to his skin. He looked as though he had been licked. His hair was neither ugly nor beautiful, so it was there for nothing, I thought.

And Grandfather's toes were very long and bent with many

lumps of hard skin. I was relieved when Grandfather kept them under the water.

When he lifted a foot to throw the sand farther away from the bank I saw how white and washed out his foot was, like something dead and washed ashore.

Unexpectedly Grandfather dropped the shovel on the shore and in a split second he lifted me out of the water. A thin black snake was moving in front of him. It was very long and thin and made waves with its body. While swimming it held its flat pointed head above the surface of the water.

It had a body like a floating branch, but it was much smoother and shinier. Grandfather had seen it from a distance.

I think it was very cold.

Grandfather blocked its way with his shovel. He hung it over his shovel's handle and threw it onto the sand on the bank.

It was beautiful and repulsive and so deadly that I was afraid for its life and couldn't wish for its death.

Grandfather hacked off its head with his shovel.

Suddenly I didn't want to be the swamp any more. My skin was dry when I timidly touched it with my fingertips.

Grandfather was still shoveling sand from the river.

Along the railroad tracks the horse was eating the tall grass. Its head and belly were sticky with burrs.

The night made the river appear deeper. There was still daylight in the valley. But the river had turned dark and the water was heavy.

Grandfather got out of the river and shoveled his sand on his wagon.

He drove the horse to the river and let it drink.

It lowered its long neck and slurped in so much water that I couldn't imagine how deep its stomach was. But I knew it was capable of drinking a whole rainfall when it was thirsty.

Now Grandfather harnessed it to the carriage and we went up the hill into the village. Water was dripping off the slats. There was a lot of water left in the sand. We left a wagon track, a water track, a sand track, and a horse track behind.

Grandmother came out of the cabbage garden with her wicker basket. Behind the sloe bushes among the scrap metal she found an old soup pot again.

She filled it with soil and planted a geranium in it.

Grandmother's geraniums were as inexpressive as paper flowers, and to Grandmother there was nothing more beautiful than geraniums in soup pots.

She had a shelf full of geraniums along the hallway, a shelf full of geraniums on the stairs next to the door to the hallway, a shelf full of geraniums next to the garden gate in the yard.

She had her living room window and kitchen window full of geraniums in soup pots. And the sand pile next to the pigpen was full of geranium seedlings. And soup pots were hanging from all the beams of the house.

Grandmother's geraniums would blossom forever.

Grandfather never said a word about them. He never said the word geranium in his life. He found geraniums neither ugly nor beautiful. They were as useless to him as the hair on his skin was useless to me. Or maybe he didn't see them at all.

When Grandfather died Grandmother carried all the geraniums she had collected into his room.

Grandfather was laid out in a forest of geraniums in soup pots. And then they were useless too. Grandfather didn't say a word about them then either.

And after his death something changed: Grandmother didn't bring any more geraniums or soup pots home.

But to this day she still has the geraniums and soup pots she had collected up to that point.

They are old now. They are ancient, and they bloom forever.

I had woken up. Grandfather was hammering again. I heard how the hammering in the yard tumbled over. For a moment everything was upside down and then fell back into itself. Even the air was noisy, even the grass was rumbling.

Now sleep was gone altogether. In the next room Grandmother was beating the warmth out of the bedding, and down feathers flew into the air and crept into her eyes.

Then Grandmother carried the full chamber pot into the back-yard and left a trail of drops in the room, in the front room, in the hallway, and in the yard. Her thumb had gotten wet too.

During the day the chamber pot would sit under the stool be-tween the couple's beds. It was covered with newspaper, and you couldn't see it, but you could smell it when you entered the room.

Every night I heard Grandmother's urine run into the chamber pot in the next room. If it didn't run with an even sound and with short interruptions I knew that Grandfather was standing above the chamber pot. Grandmother woke up every night at two-thirty, put on her felt slippers and sat down on the chamber pot. And if there was a night that she didn't wake up at two-thirty she didn't wake up till the morning, and I knew that she had fallen into a deep unhealthy sleep and that she would spend the following three days sick in bed.

Nothing would hurt her or else everything did, and she fell from sleep into half sleep and from half sleep into sleep. On the fourth day she would get up early and go right into the middle of her household, clattering about with her pots and pans into the late af-ternoon and into the hours for washing dishes, sweeping, and washing floors, and the evening descended into the weeding of the garden.

Grandmother had the most beautiful poppy in the village. It was higher than the fence and full of heavy white blossoms. When wind sprang up the long stems would hit each other, the blossoms would begin to tremble, but not a single leaf would fall to the ground.

Grandmother had those large wide blossom petals in her eyes. She weeded every thread of weed out of the flower bed.

When the heads got yellow and dry she took the biggest knife from the drawer and cut them all into a big willow basket. She would drop pots when she was cooking, plates would break in her hands, glasses would shatter on the floor in front of her, dish towels would stink and not dry from one day to the next from so much dish washing, the knife blades would get notched, the cats would doze on their chairs in the kitchen, purring and snoring. Behind her sewing needle Grandmother talked about the poppy of her childhood.

Great-grandmother, who is now hanging in a large frame above Grandmother's bed, would empty three poppy heads into Grandmother's mouth all at once. Grandmother forced down those hard seeds and fell into a deep sleep. Her parents and the hired help went out into the field and left her sleeping in the house, and when they returned late in the evening they found her still in a deep sleep.

They also used to give her crow dung that tasted like plaster, it was chalky and brittle and pungent. The pieces would pinch her tongue, and then she would fall into a long sleep as black as crows.

One day they put an especially big piece of crow dung into the mouth of Grandmother's brother, teary-eyed Franz, and he never woke up again. He had grown stiff and his face was full of blue spots. And since he didn't want to do anything but sleep anymore they buried him furtively without a funeral, without music, in a coffin made at home out of rough raw wood from the slats of a case of jam.

With his wheelbarrow the stableman took him out to the cemetery, through the dust of the streets and through the emptiness of the village. No one in the village noticed that someone had died. Even in the house no one noticed. There were still plenty of children, a room full, and an oven bench full. In the winter they went down to the village one at a time and took turns going to school because there weren't enough shoes in the house for all of their feet. No one could ever be missed by anyone in that house. If one of them wasn't there the other was.

Nowadays they have just one child in a household with seven

pairs of shoes, and even that doesn't seem like much. The house is empty, and there are those shoes, and they are shiny and clean because the child isn't allowed to walk through the dirt anymore, and if it rains they lift the child up and carry it.

Grandmother clears her throat and then doesn't say a word for hours. Sometimes she walks back and forth in the house and sings an old drinking song meaning women's eyes are cornflower blue when in tears or with wine. Once she sings it with *tears* and once she sings it with *wine*. And in her memory there are a hundred beds of poppies and all the white blossoms that ever existed in the garden wilt on her face and fall to the ground while she walks. And all the black poppy seeds trickle down from her skirts which are so heavy that she can barely walk with all the poppies.

Mother is crying. While she cries she talks as much as she cries and gets the sniffles made of water and glass, which she wipes on her sleeve.

Father is drunk again. He turns on the TV and looks at the blank screen. There is nothing but some flickering from the inside, and from that flickering you can hear some music. And Father's face is as empty as the screen, and Mother says turn off the TV, and Father just turns off the sound and lets it keep flickering, and he begins to sing a song, *Three Friends Setting Out for Life*.

With the word *Out* Father's voice gets very loud, and he points at the street through the window. The pavement is full of goose droppings. *Where did they go, in the big, big wide world?* Father's voice gets softer. They are scattered to the winds, *because no one, no one cares*. The village wind shivers above the grass and the goose droppings. Father's face, his eyes, his mouth, his ears are full of his own rough song.

The kitchen is full of steam. There is a musty smoke rising from the turnip pot to the ceiling, swallowing our faces.

We look into the hot fog which is heavy and pushes in our skulls. We look away from our loneliness, from ourselves, and can't bear the others nor ourselves, and the others next to us can't bear us either.

Father sings, and singing, Father's face falls under the table onto the stand, damn it, we are a happy family, damn it, happiness evaporates in the turnip pot, damn it, the steam bites off our heads from time to time, happiness bites off our heads from time to time, damn it, happiness eats our lives.

My face falls into Grandmother's gaping felt slippers. It is dark there, there is the big dark shelter where you don't have to breathe, there is the place where you can suffocate from yourself. Mother cries and talks. Mother talks and cries. Mother talks crying and cries talking.

While she is crying Mother manages long sentences that don't want to stop, and they would be beautiful if they didn't concern me. But they have those heavy words in them, and Father begins singing his song again, and singing he takes the knife from the drawer, the biggest knife, and I get scared of his eyes, and the knife cuts up everything I want to think.

Suddenly Mother stops talking, Father has raised the knife and is threatening. Father is singing and threatening with the knife, and now all Mother is doing is whimpering softly with her throat all clogged up.

Then she adds a white plate to the table that is already set and places a spoon on it so carefully that you can't hear when it touches the rim of the plate.

I am afraid that the table's legs will sag, that it will collapse before we can sit down at it or during dinner.

Grandfather comes in from the backyard, and dirt and grass are sticking to his shoes. Nails rattle in his coat pockets.

Grandfather's clothes are all full of nails, even the pockets of his Sunday clothes are full of nails. Once Mother found a nail even in his pajamas, and she got very angry and screamed throughout the house.

In every corner of the house there are boxes and containers with hammers and nails. When Grandfather hammers you can hear two sounds at once, one from the hammer and one from the village. The whole yard, hard as stone, echoes. The fine white teeth of the chamomile fall out. The yard feels heavy on my toes, the yard feels like a load on my feet, the yard hits my knees when I walk. The yard is hard and big and overgrown. I talk as loudly as I can, and the hammering tears the sentences from my face.

Grandfather likes to speak about his hammers and nails and even says about some people that their minds are nailed shut. Grandfather's nails are new and pointed and shiny. And his hammers are clumsy and heavy and rusty and their handles are much too thick.

Sometimes the village is a huge box made of fences and walls. Grandfather pounds his nails into it.

When you walk in the street you can hear the hammering, it sounds like woodpeckers hammering. One fence throws the sound against the other. You walk between the fences. The air trembles, the grass trembles, the blue plums breathe into the trees. And it's the height of summer, and the woodpeckers are flying around in the village. And Mother still has her hands for drudgery, and Grandmother has her poppy and hardly moves through the house anymore, and Grandfather looks after the cow and has his nails, and Father still has his drunkenness from yesterday and is drinking again today.

And Wendel hasn't learned to speak yet, and in the streets he is pelted with dust and with rocks, and pushed into puddles, and forced into ditches where the mud stinks, and the school children write on him with chalk, and he must walk through the streets with his back full of chalk marks and his face spattered with ink, and he can't go home till he cries. They don't let him go until his face is distorted with fear, until his neck is full of caterpillars and rain worms and aphids.

Wendel speaks fluently when he is alone and talking to himself. Sometimes I hear him in the backyard. We sit at the same fence,

Wendel in his yard and I am in mine. I eat mallow fruit which makes you stupid, and Wendel eats green apricots and sometimes that gives him a high temperature. And when he is healthy he eats green apricots again and talks to himself.

I asked Mother if the fence that separates our two yards belongs to Wendel or to me. I wanted to hear that it belongs to me, I wanted to be able to chase Wendel off when he leans against the fence. But Mother said that the fence belongs to me and Wendel, and that's when I wanted to curse his side of the fence so that not a single mallow blossom would grow there. I wanted him to have only rough stiff grass.

The doctors in the city say that fear is the reason for Wendel's stuttering. At some point fear took root in him and hasn't disappeared since. Now Wendel is afraid that he doesn't have enough green apricots. He is standing on the threshing floor of our yard. We are playing husband and wife. I stick two green balls of wool into my blouse, and Wendel sticks on his mustache of green wool threads.

We play. I call him names because he is drunk, because there is no money in the house, because the cow has no food. I call Wendel a lazy dog and a pig and a tramp and a drunkard and good-for-nothing and a bum and a lecher and a son of a bitch. That's how the game goes. It's fun, and it works. Wendel sits there not saying anything.

Wendel has cut his hand with an old can. A lot of blood is running into the grass. I just say idiot and don't pay attention to his wound. I simply say moron.

I cook in the sand and dress and undress my dolls, I feed them sand cakes and grass blossom soup.

I push my breasts in the right place, and Wendel is sweating under his mustache. That's how the game goes.

I throw the sand pie down and trample on it with my shoes. The grass blossom soup is flying against the wall and running to the ground. With my naked doll I run into the house and lose my breasts in front of the kitchen door.

Then I lure Wendel toward me with the first green apricots, which are still half in bloom. And Wendel comes.

Again we play husband and wife.

And Grandmother calls me for the third time. She comes out. Slapping me in the face, she chases me to my afternoon nap. When her anger has passed she says that it's just so I will be big and strong. And whom will she beat after I have gotten big and strong, who will be there unable to fend off her tough hand?

I hate this afternoon nap. That hatred is keeping me company in my bed, and Grandmother darkens the room and closes the doors one by one: the living room door, the hallway door, the front door. For two hours I can't leave the darkness. I am afraid of falling asleep. Grandmother wants to put a curse on me. I am resisting her sleep as deep as poppy sleep where I am nothing, where I am dead, as long as I am asleep. Sleep is floating through the room and is already touching my skin. Everything grows deeper than I can bear. Up on the ceiling there is a lot of foam. Flocks of birds tear up the water. There is a lot of hunger in their beaks. They'll attack me, peck at my skin, and they'll scream, you are a coward and empty. I'll wake up without a soul and without fear.

Sleep presses its muff into my face. It smells like Grandmother's skirts, like poppies and death. Sleep is Grandmother's sleep, Grandmother's poison. Sleep is death.

And I tell him that I am still a child. It has been quite often that I've wanted to die, but it didn't work then. And now we are at the height of summer, and flocks of birds tear up the water. And now I don't want to die, now I've gotten used to myself and cannot lose myself. I turn up my blanket. A lot of cool air touches my sweat. The bed is so wide and big, the bed is so white and empty that I am lying in the middle of a snow field, in the middle of a frosty night, in the middle of freezing.

The door to the yard squeaks, the hallway door creaks, the front room door groans, the door to my room bangs against the closet. Grandmother is in my room. She rumbles up the roller blinds. It's bright daylight outside. The poultry's feathers are steaming with summer.

Wendel sits on the barn floor and ties on his mustache and holds out the two balls of wool for me. Without speaking I stick them under my dress. We are playing husband and wife again. We are never finished.

At the end of the street, the sun is setting in a red pool of weariness. The village is standing there like a huge box of fence and wall. A sack, a sewed-up sack of night is descending on the village. And nothing cools down, everything grows black and heavy and elastic.

The roller blinds are creaking in their joints. Sand is drifting in the gutters. Dunes of sleep are drifting through my head. The garden gate is creaking, the wind is going through the garden beds all night long. The village has a frightening number of trees. They are all in my face.

My bed is like a cow's belly, all hot and dark and full of sweat. Grandfather's suspenders hang on a nail, and his empty pants walk through the room. When I stretch out my arm I can touch them. Perhaps there are nails in his pants pockets, you can't see them.

The mothers are asleep, the fathers are asleep, the grandmothers are asleep, the grandfathers are asleep, the children are asleep, the pets are asleep.

The village stands there like a box.

Mother doesn't cry, Father doesn't drink, Grandfather doesn't hammer, Grandmother doesn't have her poppy, Wendel doesn't stutter.

The night is not a monster, it only has wind and sleep in it.

In the next room I hear the urine rush into the chamber pot. Grandfather is standing above it. It is five o'clock.

Grandmother didn't wake up at two-thirty. She has fallen into that unhealthy sleep.

That hasn't happened for a long time.

One morning we will find her dead.

When the pools get shallow, the frogs' backs dry off. Then the heat creeps into their bellies, and all that's left of them is hard skin.

It is lying around everywhere in the yards. Only when the frogs die do we know that they live in the houses too, that they go up the stairs, up to the attics, into the black chimneys.

Our house has two chimneys, they will be full of frogs. One of the chimneys is red and the other black.

The red one is above the rooms no one lives in. Smoke never rises from it.

Many owls live in it. Every year Mother must pay chimney fees. That's quite a bit if you count all those years, says Mother, and when you think about it, one of them is there only for the owls.

Last week they were very excited. I heard them all night on the roof tiles. They have two kinds of voices, higher ones and lower ones. But even the higher ones are very low, and the lower ones are much lower.

They must be the males and females. They have a real language.

I went into the yard a few times, and I couldn't see anything but their eyes. The whole roof was full of them. They were shining, and the whole yard was bright and was glistening like ice. There was no moonlight. That night the neighbor died. The night before he had still eaten quite well. He hadn't been ill. His wife woke me up in the morning and said that he suffocated in his sleep. I immediately thought of the owls.

Between us and the neighbors the garden is full of raspberries. They are so ripe that your fingers get bloody from picking them. A few years ago we didn't have any raspberries, the neighbor just had a few bushes in his garden. Then they came over into our garden, and he doesn't have a single one left. They wander. The neighbor told me once that he hadn't planted them either, they had come by themselves from another garden. In a few years we won't have any either, they will have wandered on. Have your fill now because the village is small and they are growing their way out of the village.

Yesterday was the funeral. He had been old, but not ill. His son brought him down from the mountains some months ago. His house had collapsed, a wild creek rising over its banks had torn it down. In the mountains people are healthier. He had brought along a cap. It is neither a knit cap nor a hat. These caps are worn only in our village. He said that he wanted to be buried in that cap. He was just joking because he didn't want to die. And he wasn't ill either.

Now they've shoved that cap on his dead head. First the lid of the coffin didn't want to close so they hit it with a hammer.

Mother's legs were lying under a blanket with mine. I imagined them naked and full of varicose veins. There was a tremendous number of legs lying next to each other in the field.

Always only men lay in the war. I saw all these women lying in the battlefield with dresses slipped out of place and scraped legs. I saw Mother lying naked and frozen in Russia, with scraped legs and green lips from the turnips.

I saw Mother transparent with hunger, emaciated and wrinkled, even under her skin, like a weary unconscious girl.

Mother had fallen asleep. When she was awake I never heard her breathe. When she was asleep she would wheeze as if she still had the Siberian wind in her throat, and I felt cold next to her in my spasms of horror dreams.

Outside the water was rising in the ponds. There was no moon in the village and you couldn't see through the water and it was curdled.

The frogs were croaking from the black lungs of my dead father, from the rigid windpipe of my wheezing grandfather, from the calcified arteries of my grandmother. The frogs were croaking from all the living and the dead of this village.

Everybody brought a frog along when they immigrated. Ever since they've existed they have been praising themselves that they are Germans, and they never talk about their frogs, and they believe that whatever you refuse to talk about doesn't exist either.

Then sleep overcame me. I fell into a big pot of ink. That's how dark it had to be in the Black Forest. Outside, their German frogs were croaking.

Mother, like all the others, had brought a frog from Russia.

And I heard Mother's German frog in the back of my sleep.

ROTTEN PEARS

The gardens are intensely green. The fences are floating after moist shadows. The window panes glide bare and bright from one house to the other. The church tower is turning, the heroes' crucifix is turning. The names of the heroes are long and blurred. Käthe is reading the names from the bottom to the top. The third from the bottom is my grandfather, she says. She makes the sign of the cross in front of the church. The pond shines in front of the mill. The duckweeds are green eyes. A fat snake lives in the bulrush, Käthe says. The night watchman saw it. During the day it eats fish and ducks. During the night it slithers to the mill and eats bran and flour. The flour it leaves behind is wet from its saliva. The miller throws it into the pond because it is poisonous.

The fields are lying on their bellies. Up in the clouds the fields are standing on their heads. The sunflowers' roots tie up the clouds. Father's hands are turning the steering wheel. I can see Father's hair through the little window behind the tomato crate. The car is going fast. The village is sinking into the blue sky. I can't see the church tower any more. I see my aunt's thigh right next to Father's pant leg.

Houses fly by on the side of the road. Those houses are not villages because I don't live there. Small men, strangers, with blurred pant legs walk through the streets. The skirts of strange women are flapping on narrow rushing bridges. Under many big trees there are lonely children with bare skinny thighs without pants. They are holding apples in their hands. They are not eating. They are waving. They are shouting with empty mouths. Käthe waves back briefly and looks the other way. I wave for a long time. I look at the skinny thighs for a long time, but then they dissolve and I see only the big trees.

The plains are under the hills. The sky of our village carries the hills. They don't fall into the plains through the clouds. Now we are far away, Käthe says and yawns into the sun. Father throws a glowing cigarette out the window. My aunt moves her hands and talks.

The plums between the fences are small and green. There are cows standing in the grass looking at the dust rising from the wheels while they chew. The soil climbs up from the grass over bare rocks, over roots and bark. Käthe says: those are mountains and the stones are cliffs.

Near the wheels of the car, bushes sway with the stream of air. Water rushes from their roots. The fern drinks and shakes its lace web. The car runs on narrow gray roadways. They are called serpentines, Käthe says. The roads become snarled. Our village is way below the mountains, I say. Käthe laughs: the mountains are here, and our village is out there in the plains, she says.

The white milestones look at me. Half of Father's face is above the steering wheel. My aunt touches Father's ear.

Little birds are hopping from branch to branch. They disappear into the forest. They screech briefly. When they don't touch the branches they fly, pull their legs to their bellies and don't make a sound. Even Käthe doesn't know the names of the birds.

Käthe is looking for a small prickly cucumber in the cucumber crate. With her mouth pointed she bites into it and spits out the peels.

The sun falls behind the highest mountain. The mountain shakes and swallows the light. At home the sun sets behind the cemetery, I say. Käthe eats a big tomato and says: in the mountains, night falls earlier than at home. Käthe puts her small white hand on my knee. The car hums between Käthe's hand and my skin. In the mountains, winter comes earlier than at home too, I say.

The car's green lights are snooping through the edge of the forests. The fern spreads its lace web into the darkness. My aunt leans her cheek against the window and sleeps. Father's cigarette is glowing above the steering wheel.

The night eats the crates on top of the car, it eats the vegetables in the crates. Between the mountains the tomato smell is more pungent than at home. Käthe doesn't have arms or a face. Her hand warmly strokes my cold knee. Käthe's voice is sitting next to me speaking from a distance. I bite my lips silently so that I won't lose my mouth in the night.

The car jerks. Father turns off the green lights. He gets out of the car and shouts: we are here. The car is under a light in front of a long house. The roof of the house is black like the forest. My aunt slams the car door shut and shoves a nightshirt in Father's hands. With her bent index finger she points up into the dark and says: the village is up there. My eyes follow her index finger and I see the moon.

Here is the water mill, Käthe says. Father shoves the nightshirt under his arm and gives my aunt a key. My aunt unlocks the green front door. Käthe says: the old lady lives up there in the village with her sister.

My aunt goes behind a black door. Into her room, Father says. He goes up the narrow wooden stairs and closes the trap door behind him. In the front room Käthe and I are lying on a narrow bed below the small black window with a white lace curtain. Through the wall we hear water running. Käthe says, it's the creek.

Käthe's hair crackles in my ear. The moon is hanging in the black mouth of the clouds in front of the small black window. That's where the village is.

Käthe's thighs are lying lower than my thighs. Käthe's head is lying higher than my head. Käthe's belly breathes hot air. The straw mattress rustles under my short thin body.

The bed behind the black door crackles. The hay behind the trap door crackles.

The hot air from Käthe's belly smells of rotten pears. Käthe's breath sighs in her sleep. Dripping clumps of flowers with grasping stems and winding leaves grow from the white lace curtains.

A creak is falling down the stairs. I raise my head and drop it again. Father is following the creak. Father is barefoot. With his big hands he is groping for the black door. The door doesn't creak. Father's toes are cracking, and the black door falls shut without a sound behind his back. My aunt giggles and says: cold feet. Father smacks his lips and says: mice and hay. The bed creaks. The pillow breathes loudly. The blanket's long thrusts come quickly. Aunt is moaning, Father is panting. The bed jerks out of the wood in short thrusts.

The creek behind the house is babbling. The pebbles are pushing, the rocks are pressing. Käthe's hand twitches in her sleep. Aunt giggles, Father whispers. A round leaf flutters behind the black window.

The lock of the black door clicks. Barefoot and without his heels, Father goes up the narrow wooden stairs. His shirt is open. His walk smells of rotten pears. The trap door creaks and slowly falls shut. Käthe's face turns in her sleep. Father's thighs are crackling in the hay.

The creek babbles between my eyes: I did impure acts, I watched impure acts, I heard impure acts, I read impure acts. I dig my hands under the blanket. I draw serpentines on my thighs with my fingers. Our village is on my knee. Käthe twitches her belly in her sleep.

The flower clumps are bending their white stems. The black window has a gray tear. The clouds are hanging full of red strings. The tips of the fir needles are turning green.

Weather-beaten, my aunt is standing at the black door. Melons are trembling under her nightgown. She says something about red clouds and about wind. Käthe yawns with her big red mouth and raises her arms in front of the small window. The trap door creaks. Bent over, Father comes down the narrow stairs. His face is stubbly and he asks: had a good sleep. I say: yes. Käthe nods. My aunt buttons her blouse. The button between the melons is too small and slips out again. My aunt looks Father in the face and repeats her sentence about the wind and the red clouds. Father leans against the wooden stairs and combs his hair. He drops a clump of black hair from the greasy comb next to the stairs. We'll pick you up at two, he says. Laughing, my aunt looks at the green door and says: Käthe knows.

The car is humming. My aunt sits next to Father in the car. She combs her hair with the greasy comb. Her hair is gray behind her ears.

I look at the distant red roofs. Käthe says: the village is up there. I ask: is it big. Käthe says: small and ugly.

I lie down in the grass. Käthe sits on a rock next to the creek. I see Käthe's blue panties with the yellow stain of rotten pears between her thighs. Käthe slips her skirt between her thighs. Käthe whips the water under the rocks with a stick. I look into the water and ask: are you already a woman. Käthe throws pebbles into the water and says: you are only a woman if you have a man. And your mother, I ask. I chew up a birch leaf in my mouth. Käthe tears up a daisy and says to herself: he loves me, he loves me not. Käthe throws the bare yellow node of the daisy into the water: but my mother has children, she says. You don't have children if you don't have a man. Where is he, I ask. Käthe tears up a fern leaf: loves me, dead, loves me not. Just ask your mother if you don't believe me. I pick daisies. Old Elli has no children, I say. She never had a man, says Käthe. She crushes a brown-speckled frog with a rock. Elli is an old maid, Käthe says. Red hair is hereditary. I look into the water. Even her chickens are red and her rabbits have red eyes, I say. Small black bugs from the daisies come crawling over my hands. At night Elli sings in the garden, I say. Käthe is standing on a tree stump and calls out: she sings because she drinks. Women must get married so they won't drink. And the men, I ask. They drink because they are men, Käthe says and jumps down into the grass. They are men even if they don't have women. And your fiancé, I ask. He drinks too because they all drink, Käthe says. And how about you? I ask. Käthe rolls her eyes. I am getting married, she says. I throw a stone into the water and say: I don't drink and I won't get married. Käthe laughs: not yet, but later, you are too young now. And what if I don't want to, I say. Käthe is picking wild strawberries. When you grow up you'll want to, she says.

Käthe is lying in the grass and eating wild strawberries. Red sand sticks between her teeth. Her thighs are long and pale. The stain on Käthe's panties is wet and dark brown. Käthe throws the stripped strawberry stems over her face and sings: and that will bring to me the one I love like no one else who'll make me happy forever. Her red tongue turns and hangs on a white thread in her mouth. Elli always sings that in her garden at night, I say. Käthe shuts her mouth. How does the rest of it go, I ask. Käthe kneels in the grass waving. The car comes rolling down from the distant roofs. The empty crates are rattling on the car.

Father gets out of the car and locks the green front door. My aunt is sitting next to the steering wheel counting money. Käthe and I get into the car. The car is humming. Käthe is sitting next to me on an empty cucumber crate.

The car is going fast. I see how deep the forests are. The little birds without names flutter across the road. The shadows of the branches are jagged on Käthe's face. Käthe's lips have dark sharp edges. Her lashes are dense and pointed like fir needles.

No men, no women walk through the villages. There are no naked children standing under the big trees. There is shriveled fruit between the big trees. Shaggy dogs bark after the wheels.

The hills end in wide fields. The plains are lying on their black bellies. The wind has died down. Käthe says: we'll be home soon.

She tugs at the acacia twigs hanging down. With her white hands Käthe tears the leaves from their stems and she doesn't have a face. Her voice says softly: loves me, loves me not. Käthe chews up the bare stem in her mouth.

There is a gray church tower behind the field: there's our church, says Käthe. The village is flat and black and silent. At the village entrance Jesus hangs on the crucifix, his head is lowered and he shows his hands. His toes are thin and long. Käthe makes the sign of the cross.

The pond shimmers black and empty. The big snake eats bran and flour in the mill. The village is empty. The car stops in front of the church. I don't see the church tower. I see the long bumpy walls behind the poplar trees.

Käthe goes down the black road with my aunt. The road has no direction. I don't see the pavement. I sit down next to Father. The seat is still warm from my aunt's thighs and smells of rotten pears.

Father drives and drives. He drives his hand through his hair, he drives his tongue over his lips. Father drives through the empty village with his hands and feet.

Behind a window without a house a light is staggering. Father drives into the yard through the shadow of the gate. He pulls the canvas over the car.

Mother is sitting at the edge of the table under the light. She is darning a sock with an empty heel, she is filling it with gray wool. The wool creeps from her hand smoothly. Mother looks at Father's jacket with glances as straight as arrows. She is smiling. Her smile is weak and lame at the edges of her lips.

Father plunks down blue bills on the table and counts. Ten thousand, he says loudly. And my sister, Mother asks. Father says: she's already got her share. And eight thousand is for the engineer. Mother asks: out of that. Father shakes his head. Mother takes the money and with both hands carries it to the closet.

I am lying in my bed. Mother bends over me and kisses my cheek. Her lips are as hard as her fingers. How did you sleep there, she asks. I close my eyes: Father upstairs in the hay, Aunt in her room and Käthe and I in the front room, I say. Mother gives me a brief kiss on my forehead. Her eyes have a cold shine. She turns and leaves.

The clock is ticking through the room: I heard impure acts. My bed is between a shallow river and a weary leafy forest in the plains. Behind the wall of the room the bed creaks in short thrusts. Mother moans. Father pants. The plains are hanging full of black beds and rotten pears.

Mother's skin is flabby. Her pores are empty. The rotten pears creep back into her skin. Under my eyelids, sleep is black.

OPPRESSIVE TANGO

Mother's garter belt cuts deep into her hips and pushes her stomach over her tightly laced belly. Mother's garter is made of light blue damask with pale tulips, and it has two white rubber buttons and two fasteners made of stainless steel wires.

Mother lays the black silk stockings on the table. The silk stockings have thick sheer calves. They are black glass. The silk stockings have round opaque heels and pointed opaque toes. They are black stone.

Mother pulls the black silk stockings over her legs. The pale tulips float from her hips over her belly. The rubber buttons turn black, the fasteners close.

Mother pushes her stone toes, Mother squeezes her stone heels into her black shoes. Mother's ankles are two black stone necks.

The bell rings the same word hard and hollow. The bell rings from the cemetery. The bell strikes.

Mother carries the dark wreath of fir and white chrysanthemums. Grandmother carries the rattling wreath of white rocks with the round picture of the smiling Virgin Mary and the faded Hungarian inscription from the time of the monarchy: Szüz Mária Köszönöm, Virgin Mary, thank you. The wreath sways under Grandmother's index finger on her thin reddened joint.

I carry a bunch of tangled fine-fibered fern and a handful of candles that are as white and as cold as my fingers.

Mother's dress falls in black folds. Mother's shoes clack in short steps. Mother's tulips float around her belly.

The bell rings the same word into its stroke. There is an echo before and after and it doesn't fade out. With calves of glass, with stone ankles, Mother trips into the echo of the word, into the stroke.

Little Sepp walks ahead of Mother, with a wreath of fir and white chrysanthemums.

I walk between the dark wreath of fir and the rattling wreath of white rocks. I walk behind my tangled fern.

I walk through the cemetery gate and the bell is in front of my face. The stroke of the bell is under my hair. The stroke is in my pulse next to my eyes and in my weary wrists under the tangled fern. The knot that dangles from the rope of the bell is in my throat.

Grandmother's index finger is blue and dead at the root of the nail. Grandmother hangs her rattling wreath of white rocks on the gravestone over Father's face. In place of Father's deep eyes there is now the smiling Mary's red heart, bared of flesh. Where Father's tight lips are there is now the Hungarian inscription from the monarchy.

Mother bows over the dark wreath of fir. Her stomach gets pushed down over her belly.

The white chrysanthemums roll up on Mother's cheeks. Mother's black dress billows up in the wind that sweeps over the graves. Mother's black glass foot has a thin white crack that goes across her thigh to the rubber button, to Mother's belly where the tulips float.

With her dead index finger, Grandmother is plucking at the tangled fern lying at the edge of the grave. I put the white candles between its ribs and stick my cold fingertips into the soil.

The match is flickering blue in Mother's hand. Mother's fingers are trembling and the flame is trembling. The soil is eating the knuckles off my fingers. Mother carries the flame around the grave and says: one doesn't poke around in graves. Grandmother points her dead index finger the other way and points at the smiling Mary's red heart, bared of flesh.

The pastor is standing on the steps to the chapel. Black folds are hanging over his shoes. The folds are creeping over his belly under his chin. The rope for the bell, the thick knot, is dangling behind his head. The pastor says: let's pray for the living and the dead souls, and he folds his bony hands over his belly.

The fir folds its needles, the fern bends its tangled ribs. The chrysanthemums have the scent of snow, the candles have the scent of ice. The air above the graves turns black and hums a prayer: Lord God, heavenly host, deliver us from this exile. Above the tower of the chapel, the night is as black as Mother's glass feet.

The candles press a trickling maze from their fingers. The air makes the trickling maze as rigid as my ribs. The wicks are crumbly charcoal and don't sustain the flames. A clump of soil rolls under the fern between the bent candles.

The rolled-up chrysanthemums are on Mother's forehead and she says: one doesn't sit on graves. Grandmother extends her dead index finger. The tear on Mother's glass leg is as wide as Grandmother's dead index finger.

The pastor says: dear faithful, today is All Saints' Day, today our dearly departed, our dead souls rejoice. Today our dead souls have their festival.

Little Sepp, with folded hands, is bowing over the wreath of evergreen at the neighboring grave: Oh Lord, deliver us from this exile. His gray hair is quivering in the quivering light.

With his red accordion, little Sepp plays the white flowing brides through the village, he plays the paired-up wedding guests with their white waxen bows around the altar, under the smiling Mary's red heart, bared of flesh, he plays the vanilla cake with the two white waxen doves on top in front of the bride's face. With his red accordion, little Sepp plays the oppressive tango for the arms and legs of the men and women.

Little Sepp has short fingers and short shoes. He presses the keys with his short fingers spread apart. The wide keys are snow, the narrow ones earth. Little Sepp rarely pushes the narrow keys. When he pushes them the music goes cold.

Father's thighs press against Mother's belly, surrounded by floating pale tulips.

The flowing bride is our neighbor. She waves her index finger. She cuts a sliver of the cake for me and, with a despondent smile, puts the white waxen doves in my hand.

I close my hand. The doves are getting as warm as my skin and they are sweating. I stick the white waxen doves into a meat dumpling and into the bread and I take a bite of it. I swallow the bread and hear the oppressive tango.

Mother dances by the edge of the table, with floating tulips and Uncle's thighs.

Around her mouth are the rolled-up chrysanthemums and she says: one doesn't play with food.

The pastor raises his bony hands in the name of the Lord: deliver us from our exile. A trickling maze of smoke rises from his hands and drifts around the knot on the bell rope and rises into the tower.

The grave has sunk, Mother says. We need two cart loads of soil on it and one cart load of fresh manure to make the flowers grow. Mother's black shoes grind on the sand. Your uncle had better do that for his dead brother, Mother says.

Grandmother hangs the wreath with the white rocks from her dead index finger.

Father's sunken eyes look at Mother's black glass foot with the white tear. Mother's black shoes are walking across mole hills between unfamiliar graves.

We walk through the cemetery gate. The village caves in and smells of evergreen and fern, of chrysanthemums and of a waxen maze.

Little Sepp is walking ahead of me.

The village is black. The clouds are like black damask.

Grandmother rattles the wreath of white rocks. Mother squashes my fingers in her hand.

Father is our dead soul. Father is having a festival today and he is dancing alongside the village.

Mother's garter cuts deep into her hips.

In the oppressive tango, Father thrusts his thighs against a cloud of black damask.

THE WINDOW

Mother is pulling the eighth lace around my hips. The laces are white and tight. The laces are hot and squeeze my hips and squash the breath in my throat.

Peter is sitting on a chair at the corner of the table waiting.

The petticoats are folded in stony pleats and trimmed with lace. The holes in the lace, the narrow ribbing is musty and heavy. The lace has chalky veins like the long walls with chalky veins in the old mill.

The ninth petticoat is light gray like the plums in the morning. It is floating on the stone petticoats. I feel only its hot string. The ninth petticoat has white flowers on a silky gray dusky background. The flowers are little bells with their heads bowed. There are many heads hidden in the pleats. You can see them only when I whirl, when the accordion squeaks, when the black clarinet screams, when the stretched calfskin hums on the drum.

Peter whirls me around his face.

The white bells get dizzy and rustle a beat. My shoes step a beat, the fringes of my shawl fumble a beat. My hair flies a beat. One curl falls over my ear, one curl falls on my neck, one curl falls on the root of my nose and smells of mashed plums. The hum of the drum is as hollow as a bridge.

Tony whirls half his face behind Barbara's head. My eyes whirl past Tony's ears. My ears whirl around Peter's head.

The calfskin hums on my temples, on my elbows, and on my

knees. The calfskin hums under my shawl, under my skin, and clamps down on my heart.

My hips are hot, my thighs are taut, my muscles whirl on my belly.

There are four scarves with flying fringes between Tony and me. There is the face of the baker and his black clarinet between Tony and me.

My petticoats are swaying around my calves. My silky gray skirt is whirling around Peter's pantlegs. The white bells pull their heads out of the pleats. My silky gray skirt is a silent bell.

Peter's thighs are hot and throbbing. Peter's knees are hard and pointed. Peter's eyes gleam in front of my face. Peter's mouth shimmers red and moist. Peter's hand is big and hard. Tony raises Barbara's hand under his ear.

The black clarinet is silent. The baker shakes the spit out of it. The baker sings: dance with me through the night. Peter presses his hard white shirt collar against my neck.

I close my eyes and dance with Tony and my silky gray skirt to the edge of the village, behind the mill, behind the last thread of the high bulb's white light, under the hollow bridge.

My blouse is soft, its buttons are small, its buttonholes are big. My skirt is like dusk and rises like fog. Tony's hands burn on my belly. My knees float apart and swim as far as my thighs are long. My belly twitches, my temples press down on my eyes. The bridge is hollow and groans, and its echo falls into my mouth. Tony pants and the grass sighs. My skirt rises under my elbows. Tony's back is sweating on my hands. Up there in the moon, behind my hair, forgotten dogs bark and the night guard is leaning on the long wall of the chalky veins of the old mill and he sleeps. The bridge whirls around my hands, and my tongue turns in Tony's mouth. With faltering breath Tony digs a hole into my belly. My knees are floating to the edge of the bridge. The bridge falls into my eyes. Hot slime flows into my belly and spreads over me, and seals up my breath and buries my face.

I open my eyes. There are quivering drops on my forehead. The weary rain under the hollow bridge runs down my throat.

Peter squashes my hand with his big thumb, with his sticky sweat. Peter whirls me around him and whirls around me. I am floating around Peter and my knees are of lead.

The baker shakes the spit out of his black clarinet and sings with a skipping voice: oh no, oh no, she said, no kiss for me. His eyes swirl like the wine in a jug. Tony's black shoulders turn around Barbara's flying fringes.

Peter makes a window with me. My fingers stick to Peter's fingers. My arms wind around his elbows. The window twists out of his flesh and my squashed hands in front of my face. Through the window I see half of Tony's face.

Between our windows, between our half faces there is my mother's angular face with her black silk scarf, with speckled piercing eyes and a toothless mouth.

Those piercing eyes swim out of the angular face, out of the black silk scarf, swim to the end of the open road, to the end of the bound-up village. Behind the last gardens, behind the hollow bridge, the piercing eyes break the soil and fall in.

There is a crucifix at the edge of the village. Jesus hangs on the side of the road bleeding and looks disinterested into the turnip fields through a window of broken plum trees.

My eyes swim out of the window, swim out of my head, out of my hot mouth, out of my hidden sweat. My window is blind. My arms are folded as in death in Peter's arms. Once again I look through my blind window and say quickly and softly: I am not feeling well.

My tongue falls into my mouth. I stumble over my silky gray dusky bell. I sink down into the agitated pleats of the black skirts of ancient women, into their clutching hands, into their toothless mouths.

The black skirts are as open as the streets, as tied up as the village, as broken as the clutching earth behind the last gardens, behind those piercing eyes, behind those toothless mouths.

THE MAN WITH THE MATCHBOX

Every night the village burns down. First the clouds burn.

Every summer takes a barn down with it. It's always on Sundays when people are dancing and playing cards that the barns burn down. Dusk surges through the streets like a large intestine. Then there is a smoldering deep down in the straw and the stalks. And there is only one person in the know, the man with the matchbox who carries his hatred through the potato foliage, behind the cornfields. As a frail boy he had to haul big bags and hoe turnips in this garden. At this house he slept in the barn. At this house he was called a stable boy by a girl his age who had smooth blond braids, who ate oranges in the winter and who squirted the fragrant juice of the empty peels into his face. Now he walks through the corn, and there is a rustle behind him so that he himself believes he is the wind.

Out on the road, the fat man still follows him with his small severe eyes, and in the pub he sits at a different table and only now and then looks at his face through the crook of his arm.

Now the flames lash out, now they roll up to the roof shingles with their red hot skirts. And in the sky over the village the embers are ablaze.

Fire, someone shouts, then two shout, then everybody shouts the same word, and the village totters on the hill. The men come running with buckets.

Firefighters come from their firefighters' festival with their red-painted pump on wheels, which stretches its squeaking rotating arm into the trees. There is crackling and sparkling around the big glowing barn. Then there is a crash, and the beams break and collapse. And the kettle gets hot, and the faces get red and black and swollen with fear.

I am standing in the backyard, my legs grow out of my throat. All I have is that choked-up throat. My throat jumps over the fences.

The fire tortures me with its tongs. The fire comes closer, and my legs are black charcoal.

I am the one who set the fire. Only the dogs know that. Every night they roam through my sleep. They say they won't tell on me, but they will bark me to death.

Men came rushing into our yard. They emptied the milk into the garden and took the buckets with them, and dragged my father along by his sleeves and said, come, you are also part of the fire department, and you too have a nice hat and a dark red uniform. My father took their cry in his mouth and ran after them. My father took their fear into his eyes. And his dark red uniform ran ahead of him on the pavement. And at every step his nice hat took a bite out of his thick hair. There was hot sweat on my forehead, the red waves under my eyelids burned my eye.

I run through the grass. The crowd is standing there gawking. And so am I.

I sense their piercing eyes on my neck.

And always next to me is the man with the matchbox.

His elbow, next to my arm his elbow. It is hard and pointed.

Garden soil crumbles off his shoes.

No one looks at me. They all just consist of backs and heels and apron bows and tips of scarves.

Everyone is hushed.

And they are still hushed, but they are shutting me out.

And he wins the card game on Sunday. And he dances beautifully, the man with the matchbox.

VILLAGE CHRONICLE

Ever since the village has only had eleven students and four teachers, together called the grade school, the P.E. teacher also has to teach agriculture. Ever since then, in agriculture class, they've practised the long jump in a sandpit that is always wet, and they've played Völkerball, with balls in the summer and snowballs in the winter. In this game, students divide themselves into nations. Anyone hit by the ball has to step back behind the line of fire, and since he is dead, he has to watch until all the rest of his people have been shot, which in the village is called killed in action. The P.E. teacher has a difficult time dividing the students. That's why after each class he writes down which nation each student belonged to. If you were allowed to be a German during the last class you must be a Russian the next class, and if you were a Russian the last class you are allowed to be a German the next one. Occasionally the teacher can't manage to convince enough students to be Russians. If the teacher gets desperate he says, O.K., you're all Germans and let's go. But then the students don't understand why they should fight, so they divide themselves into Saxons and Swabians.

During the summer the students even bring red ink and paint red spots on their skin and shirts after they've been shot.

The P.E. teacher, who is also the principal and the music teacher and the German teacher, has also taken on the history class a few days ago because this game is appropriate for history lessons too.

Right next to the school is the preschool. The children sing songs and recite poems. The songs deal with hiking and hunting and the poems are about love for Mother and Fatherland. Sometimes the preschool teacher, who is very young, called young filly in the village, and plays the accordion very well, even teaches the children some hits with English words like darling and love in them. Sometimes it happens that the boys grab the girls under their skirts or peek through the wide crack at the door to the girls' bathroom, all of which the preschool teacher calls a disgrace. Since this happens from time to time there are parent-teacher conferences, which are called consultations in the village. In these parent-teacher conferences the preschool teacher gives the parents instructions, which is called advice in the village, on how to punish their children. The most commonly recommended punishment, suitable for any offense, is grounding. After the children have returned home from preschool they may not leave the house for one or two weeks.

The marketplace is next to the preschool. Years ago sheep, goats, cows, and horses were bought and sold in the marketplace. Now once every spring, a few muffled-up men come from neighboring villages bringing wooden crates with piglets on their wagons. The piglets are bought and sold only in pairs. Prices depend less on their weight than their breed, called race in the village. The buyers bring along a neighbor or a relative to inspect the piglets' build, called stature in the village: whether they have short or long legs, ears, snouts, bristles, whether they have curled or straight tails. The black-spotted piglets and the piglets with varied eye colors, which are called bad-luck piglets in the village, have to be crated up and taken back by the seller if he doesn't want to sell them at half price.

Aside from piglets the villagers also breed rabbits, bees, and poultry. Poultry and rabbits are called small animals in the newspapers, and the people who raise poultry and rabbits are called small-animal breeders.

Aside from pigs and small animals the villagers also have dogs and cats that have become indistinguishable because they have interbred for decades. The cats are even more dangerous than the dogs, they interbreed even with rabbits, which is called mating in the village.

The village elder who has survived two world wars and then some other things and some other people, had a big red tomcat. Three times in a row, his female rabbit gave birth to red-and-gray-spotted litters that were meowing and that he drowned each time. After the third time the village elder hanged his tomcat. After that his female rabbit twice gave birth to striped litters, and after the second time the neighbor hanged his striped tomcat. The last time, his female rabbit had long-haired curly young ones in her nest because some tomcat from a neighboring alley or a neighboring village, a cross between a village dog and a village cat, has hair like that. Since by this time the village elder had reached his wit's end, he slaughtered his rabbit and buried her because he didn't want to eat the meat since she'd had cats in her belly for years. The whole village knows that the village elder ate cat meat as a prisoner of war in Italy. But the village elder says that this in no way means that he has to put up with his rabbit's incest since a Swabian village after all, thank God, is not in Italy, he insists, although sometimes he has the impression it could be in Sardinia. But the villagers attribute this impression to his arterial sclerosis and say that the blood in his head has thickened.

Next to the marketplace is the People's Council, which is called the Assembly Hall in the village. The building is a combination of a farmhouse and a village church. You can tell it's part farmhouse by its open veranda surrounded by a balustrade held up by posts, the small dusky windows, the brown roller blinds, and the pink-coated walls and the green-coated base. The village church shows in the four flights of steps at the entrance, the arch above the door, the wooden double door with a grate, the quiet of the rooms, and the owls and bats in the attic, called vermin in the village.

The mayor, called judge in the village, holds his meetings in the

Assembly Hall. Among those attending are smokers who are smok-ing absentmindedly; non-smokers who are not smoking but sleep-ing; alcoholics, called boozers in the village, who keep bottles un-der their chairs; as well as non-alcoholics and non-smokers who are feebleminded, which is called respectable in the village, who pre-tend that they are listening but are thinking about something to-tally different provided they are capable of thinking.

Even strangers who come to the village visit the People's Council because when they have the urge they go to the backyard for a piss, which is called passing water in the village. The toilet in the back-yard of the People's Council is a public bathroom since it has nei-ther door nor roof. Despite the many similarities between the Peo-ple's Council and the church, it has never happened that a stranger went into the church instead of the People's Council. After all you can tell the church by its crucifix and the People's Council by its memorial plaque, called the honors box in the village. The honors box displays newspapers that are replaced when they have turned totally yellow and illegible.

Next to the People's Council is the barber shop, called the bar-ber's parlor in the village. In the barber's parlor there is a chair in front of a mirror, a coal stove in one corner, and a wooden bench along a wall where customers, called shaving guests in the village, sit and sleep, which is called waiting in the village.

There is no one older than a hundred among the shaving guests. Besides getting shaved all the guests also have their hair cut, even those who don't have any hair left. The barber, called a shaver in the village, sharpens his razor after each shave on a strop that starts swinging and humming. He rubs the faces of the younger shaving guests, those under seventy, with perfume and the older ones with alcohol because it isn't proper, called fitting in the village, that an old man smells of perfume, which is called reeking of perfume in the village.

Next to the barber shop and in front of the People's Council, a concrete slab was poured, called the country fairgrounds in the village. The country fair couples dance on this concrete slab.

Since the village keeps getting smaller and smaller because people are going, if not somewhere else, at the very least to the city, the country fairs have been getting bigger and bigger and the folk costumes more and more festive. So the newspapers can't get around describing in detail every country fair in every village, which in the newspapers is called a township at the very least, if not a major township. Since in every village every country fair, called country festival in the village, is held on a different Sunday, all the country fair couples go to the country fairs of neighboring villages before or after their own country fair, and they call that joining in the village. But since in the Banat region all villages are neighboring villages, all the country fairs have the same couples participating, the same audience, and the same band. Thanks to the country fairs the young people all over the Banat know each other, and so there are often marriages between villages if parents can actually be convinced that while they may not be from the same village they are Germans after all.

Next to the barber shop there is the cooperative store, called the emporium in the village. It is five square meters large and carries pots, scarves, jam, salt, fustian fabric, slippers, and a stack of books from the early sixties. The sales clerk has diabetes and probably comes from the neighboring village because there is someone named Kondi there and Franziska is a common name.

In our village the women's names are Magdalena, which is Leni in village language, or Theresia, which is Resi in the village. The men in our village have names like Matthias, which is Matz in the village, or Johann, which is Hans in the village. Family names in our village are occupations: Schuster (shoemaker), Schneider (tailor), Wagner (cartwright), and animals: Wolf, Bär (bear), Fuchs (fox). In addition to these names there are two more names in our village: Schauder (shudder) and Stumper (bungler), and no one knows where they come from. Some so-called linguists from the Banat proved through so-called linguistic research that these names came from corruptions of other names. Aside from these names there are also mocking names in the village, called nicknames: Schmalzbauer (lardfarmer), Geizhals (miser).

Next to the cooperative store is the Cultural Center. The Cultural Center is where the country fair is held when it is raining, and weddings when it is raining, hailing, snowing, or nice. The Cultural Center has four flights of stairs as well, a heavy wooden door with just a lattice to see through, an arched entryway, small dusky windows, brown roller blinds, and vermin in the attic. A large stove, called a kitchen range in the village, with a big built-in boiler has been installed in a small pitch-dark room where the projector for the movie theater used to be, since no one goes to the movies any more, but weddings have become more and more frequent. Ever since the rotten floor was replaced by hardwood, even the older wedding guests, called wedding couples in the village, once again dance the polka instead of the waltz or foxtrot.

Next to the Cultural Center is the post office. The post office has two employees: the postman, called the mail carrier in the village, and the telephone operator, called the postwoman in the village, and she is the postman's wife. Since the postwoman is very rarely on the phone she puts postmarks on incoming mail and on outgoing mail in the evening after emptying the mailbox. The postwoman knows all the letters inside out and therefore she knows everything about the most intimate thoughts of the villagers.

Next to the post office is the militia. The militiaman, called the blue guy in the village, from time to time goes to a small room, called an office in the village, where there is an empty desk and a chair, then goes to the window to air out the room till he is done smoking his imported cigarette, then he closes the window, hangs the lock on the door and goes to the post office. Then he sits for hours with the postwoman behind the high counter and talks.

The village has three side alleys, called back alleys in the village, since one of them is behind the school and ends at the LPG,* another one is behind the cooperative store and ends at the state-owned farm, and the third is behind the post office and ends at the cemetery.

The side alleys are rows of houses. The houses in these rows all have the same pink coat, the same green base, and the same brown roller blinds. The only difference is the numbers on the doors. In the early morning before it's fully light, you can hear the hens clucking and the geese cackling and hissing in the side alleys. When it's fully light outside, called as light as day in the village, the voices of the women, called housewives in the village, talking to each other across fences and gardens, called chatting in the village, rise above the clucking, cackling, and hissing. The gardens are always newly hoed and weeded, which is called neat in the village.

The houses in the village are clean. The housewives spend their days cleaning, wiping, sweeping, and brushing, which is called domestic and thrifty in the village. On Saturdays, the Persian rugs, which are as big as half the yard and called Persians in the village, hang over fences. They get beaten, brushed, combed, and then put back into the drawing room, called the extra room in the village. The extra room has dark polished furniture made of cherry or basswood with walnut or rosewood veneer.

On the furniture there are knickknacks, called figurines in the village, and they represent various animals, from bugs and butterflies to horses. Lions, giraffes, elephants, and polar bears are especially popular since these animals don't exist in the Banat area, called the Banatland in newspapers and homeland in the village. But those animals live in different countries, which are called foreign countries in the village.

For years the village elder has longed to visit a friend from his days as a prisoner of war in a foreign country, called the West in the village, because he wanted to see a real lion.

---

*Landwirtschaftliche Produktionsgenossenschaft, a producers' cooperative in socialist countries.

The windows are covered by white nylon curtains, called lace curtains in the village. Many housewives have their lace curtains brought in from relatives in foreign countries and pay for the beautiful present with a few kilos of homemade sausage or a smoked ham. They say those curtains are really worth it since the rooms are never used, which is called saved in the village, and so will be kept for their children and grandchildren.

The houses have yards divided in two, called backyards and front yards in the village. In the front yards there are colorful garden gnomes and big green tree frogs, called garden frogs in the village, standing under a huge grape arbor and between the trimmed velvet rose bushes. In the backyard you find the poultry and the dark steamy places where the villagers cook, eat, do laundry and ironing, and sleep, called summer kitchens in the village. The villagers divide the week into meat and starch days depending on the menu. The villagers eat greasy food with salt and pepper. But if the village doctor tells them they can't eat grease, salt, and pepper, they eat without grease, salt, and pepper and say while eating that there is nothing more important than your health and that life is no longer fun when you can't eat what you want any more, and: *Tasty Fare, Good-bye Care.*

Behind the side alleys are the fields of the LPG and the state-owned farm. The fields are large and flat. In the winter the plants suffer from frost, called freeze-to-death in the village, in the spring from sogginess, called rot-to-death in the village, in the summer from heat, called scorch-to-death in the village. And in the fall, harvest time is a rainy period, called the harvest campaign in the newspapers, which in the newspapers is over in October and in the village is not even over by December. The deep holes you can see in the fields in the winter are not furrows made by ploughs, but the footmarks of the peasants who sink into the ground deeper than their boot tops during the harvest. Some peasants say that there hasn't been a true harvest since nationalization, which is called expropriation in the village. The peasants say that since expropriation even the best soil isn't worth anything, and the village elder claims that there is a huge difference between the soil of the backyard garden and the field, such a huge difference as if it had never been the same soil.

The land around the village is the land of the LPG and the state-owned farm. The land of the LPG is behind the first back alley, and the land of the state-owned farm is behind the second back alley.

The LPG consists of a chairman who is the mayor's brother, four engineers, one of whom is responsible for weeding, one for the seven cows and eleven pigs, one for the three hectares of cucumbers and two hectares of tomatoes, and one for the three tractors, and then there are seven LPG peasants who are over fifty and who are called members in the village and who are addressed as boys and girls by the engineers. In meetings the engineers attribute bad harvests and the debts of the LPG to the soil, which is too sandy for the grain and not sandy enough for the vegetables. The soil is good for the thistles and bindweed which suffocate the grain and vegetables, called crops by the engineers. The engineer in charge of weeding says that the soil of the LPG is too acid and sticky.

The state-owned farm consists of a chairman, called director in the village, who is the mayor's brother-in-law and the LPG chairman's brother; five engineers, one of whom is in charge of the nine cows and fifteen pigs, one in charge of the six hectares of carrots and ten hectares of potatoes, one in charge of the grain, and one the orchard, called the tree nursery in the village; and then there are one hundred laborers who live in the abandoned chicken coops of the state-owned farm. The engineers attribute the bad harvests of the state-owned farm to the soil, which is too briny for grain and not briny enough for the vegetables and the fruit trees. The soil is good for poppies and cornflowers, which shine bright in the field and are flashy in the pictures too, as the engineers say. The former engineer who was in charge of weeding got first prize, called won in the village, for a color photograph at a friendship exhibit of Romanian and Bulgarian photographers in Craiova, thanks to these flashy colors of the poppies and the cornflowers. The prize was a trip to Italy. Ever since that trip the brigadier, who is the cousin of the mayor, the LPG chairman, and the state farm director, has been in charge of weeds.

The cemetery is behind the third back alley. The cemetery has a blackthorn hedge and a heavy black iron gate. At the end of the main street is the chapel that is a small version of the village church and looks like a summer kitchen in better circles.

The chapel was built, called donated in the village, before the first world war by the butcher who after surviving the war went to Rome where he saw the Pope, called the Holy Father in the village. His wife, who was a seamstress but who was also called a butcher in the village, died a few days after the chapel was finished and was buried, which is called laid to rest in the village, in the family vault under the chapel.

Under the chapel there are snakes in addition to worms and moles, which are everywhere in the cemetery. Because of his revulsion against the snakes the butcher is still alive today, and he has become the village elder.

All those who are dead are lying in graves, called resting in the village, except for the butcher woman. The village dead ate themselves to death or drank themselves to death, called worked themselves to death in the village. The exceptions are the heroes, in which case you can assume that they fought themselves to death. There are no suicides in the village since all the villagers have good common sense that they don't lose even in their old age.

In order to prove that the heroes have not died in vain, which in the village is called finding a hero's death, probably because you can assume they looked for it, they are buried twice in the same cemetery: once in the family grave and once under the memorial crucifix. But in actuality they lie somewhere else in a mass grave, which is called remaining in the war in the village. Those killed in action usually have white or gray obelisks on their grave mounds. Those among the dead who used to be landowners now have white marble crucifixes above their heads. Their day laborers, called farmhands in the village, get tin-plated metal crucifixes, and the young unmarried servant girls, called domestics in the village, get black-stained crucifixes above their dead heads. This way when dead people get buried in the cemetery you can tell if their ancestors, called forebears in the village, were masters or servants.

The biggest crucifix is the memorial crucifix. It is higher than the chapel. Engraved on it are the names of all the heroes from all fronts of all wars, even those missing in action, called deported in the village.

I close the black cemetery gate behind me. Behind the cemetery there is the field, which is called pasture in the village. There are a few trees in the pasture.

I climb a tree on the edge of the field although it could just as well be in the center of the village, and maybe it really is in the center of the village. I hold onto a branch with both hands and can see the church of the neighboring village where on the third step a ladybug is cleaning its right wing.

ABOUT GERMAN MUSTACHES
AND HAIR PARTS

Recently a friend in a nearby village came back home. He wanted to visit his parents there. There's twilight in the village all day, he said. There is neither day nor night. There is neither dusk nor dawn. The twilight is in people's faces.

He didn't recognize anyone although he had lived in that village for many years. All the people had the same old gray faces. He groped his way past those faces. He greeted them and didn't get an answer. He constantly ran into walls and fences. Sometimes he walked through houses that were built right across the road. All the doors slammed shut behind him, creaking. When there was no door ahead of him he knew that he was in the street again. People talked but he didn't understand their language. He couldn't even tell if they were walking close to him or far away, or if they were moving toward or away from him. He heard a cane knock at a wall and asked a man where his parents could be found. The man said a long sentence in which several words rhymed and pointed into space with his cane.

There was a sign under a light bulb that said *Barber Shop*. The barber emptied a tin bowl of water and white foam through the door into the street. My friend entered the room. Old men were sitting on benches and sleeping. As soon as it was their turn the barber called their names. Some of those who were asleep woke up from that call and they all shouted together the name called out.

The man called woke up, and while he was sitting down in the chair in front of the mirror the others fell asleep again.

German part? the barber asked.

The man asked nodded and looked into the mirror silently. The men on the benches seemed to sleep without breathing. They sat there as rigid as corpses. You could hear the scissors.

The barber emptied the tin bowl through the door into the street. My friend was standing close to the gush of water. He was leaning with his back on the door frame. The barber pursed his lips as if he were going to whistle. He didn't whistle. Sternly he looked into the faces of those sleeping. Then he clicked his tongue. Suddenly the barber was calling out the name of my friend's father. Some men woke up and together said his father's name with wide open eyes. A man with a gray face and a black twisted mustache rose and went to the chair. The men on the benches fell asleep again.

German part? the barber asked.

German mustache and German part, the man said. You could hear the scissors, and the twisted tips of his mustache fell to the floor.

On tiptoes my friend went toward the chair. Father, he said, and the man in the chair stared stubbornly into the mirror. He tapped his shoulder with his hand. The man in front of the mirror was staring even more stubbornly into the mirror. The barber held the scissors wide open in the air. He turned his spread-out hand and rotated the scissors once around his thumb. My friend went back to his place and was again leaning his back against the door frame. With his fingers spread, the barber lathered the whiskers of the man in the chair. In front of the mirror, gray dust was floating between the faces. The barber emptied his tin bowl through the door into the street. The man slipped out the door right next to the gushing water. On tiptoes my friend went into the street. The man walked ahead of him—or was it a different man? Twilight was right in his face. He couldn't see anymore if the person was coming toward him or going away from him. Then he noticed that the man was walking away from him, but his walking away looked like a dropping off although the road was even. My friend ran into several fences and walls. He walked to the railway station through several houses that were built right across the road.

He had a bad backache when he walked and knew that he had been leaning against the door frame for a long time. He felt a strong pain in his fingers and knew that he had pushed open a lot of doors. When the train approached the railway station he felt a strong pain in his throat and knew that all that time he had been talking to himself.

He didn't see the stationmaster. But the stationmaster gave a long and shrill whistle. The train made a lot of wind when it came close. The train gave a short and hoarse whistle. Between the twilight and the steam of the train there was a tree close to the tracks. The tree was dried up. That sign was still on its trunk. From the moving train my friend saw that on that sign it didn't say the name of the village like it used to but simply RAILWAY STATION.

THE INTERVILLAGE BUS

Gerlinde, why do you let him drink like that, you are sitting next to him, aren't you, shouted a woman who was standing in the front, right behind the driver. A fat mute child looked up. Where is your mind, Franz, she said to a man with bright red cheekbones whose one hand was holding onto the rod of the baggage rack and whose other hand, without a nail on his index finger, passed through his hair to his neck.

See how you're sweating, giving you a clean shirt is all for nothing, even then you're not really human.

In the baggage rack the chrysanthemums, wrapped in newspaper, were quivering. Around the curves, dull stiff blossoms would break off.

Those flowers are just what we needed, those typical Wallachian flowers, they stink so much they make you sick, a woman said.

Those Swabian women fill the whole bus with their cackling, a man said.

A gypsy was sitting on the spare tire and was putting pumpkin seeds into the left corner of his mouth and spitting the shell out the right one.

Those guys will eat anything. Yesterday there were three of them in the village with a black car. All three of them in suits. They were gathering dead chickens, they heard about the chicken disease. All but three of my mother's died on her. You can't tell from looking at them. They cackle and keel over and are dead. Those guys have cars, people like us never have that kind of money. People like us don't eat dead chickens, but we are always sick, even if we eat without salt and without pepper and without sugar and without fat.

Yesterday afternoon my husband was at the barber's, these days he's the one pulling teeth in the village. The dentist won't come any more. Rotten teeth is a village disease, he said, even children have rotten canines.

A hundred lei for every tooth, that's enough, I said, all those bridges in your mouth, let him pull them all out and get dentures, I said.

Franz, will you put that schnapps bottle away, will you. That booze has done in a lot of people.

You can't tell them anything, mine could still be alive, but they just won't listen.

It's better when they kick the bucket, then you have your peace.

Yeah, but they don't die until they have eaten up your life.

Blood-red grape juice was dripping from the baggage rack on someone's head. It had licked a sticky hole, like a nest, in the middle of the head. Whose bag is that, said the guy who got the juice dripping on his head, and no one said a word.

He pushed the window open and threw the bag out of the window.

What an asshole, a woman said in an undertone, and when he looked at her she said loudly, the bag doesn't belong to me, but you are an asshole anyway.

On one side the curtains were drawn. The sky was red and that hurt your eyes.

The fat mute child was nibbling at her braid, and the woman next to her saw that and said ugh. The child looked the other way and bit deeper into her braid.

The bus was rumbling past bright red walls that didn't have

windows but company shingles with big black letters and big black periods. And they would never come out as a word.

Their fences are red too, one man said.

Yesterday during the night shift, a boy got his hands cut off by the five-ton press. The foreman fired a mechanic and gave him a bottle of schnapps and then screwed in the missing light bulbs. In the changing-room they caught the mechanic pouring schnapps into the boy. They pounced on the mechanic, he is in the hospital now.

The fat mute child was leaning her head against the window pane and was babbling to herself. She bit her tongue when the bus went over a pothole. She cried and babbled.

The corn is lying in the field rotting. The big pigs have eaten the tails off the piglets. They say it's a disease or incest.

In the spring there was a lot of snow melt, more than it had snowed. So all the sheep died except a few that had been slaughtered earlier. They had brain tumors. The shepherd died of weariness.

Franz, why do you let her eat beans, you are standing right next to her after all.

Spit them out, Gerlinde, they are stolen, the man said.

The fat mute child quickly swallowed and looked bored into the big bag that was filled with beans. The agronomist closed the bag's zipper.

A woman laughed nervously. They learn how to steal at universities, she said. Franz, put on her jacket.

Come on, Gerlinde, the man said, you can't find the sleeve.

The gypsy on the spare tire put on his socks and slipped into his shoes.

The driver looked at the empty bus and got a hiccup.

Close your buttons, Gerlinde, a woman said.

MOTHER, FATHER, AND THE LITTLE ONE

Greetings from the sunny coast of the Black Sea. We had a good trip here. The weather is beautiful. The food is good. The cafeteria is downstairs in the hotel, and the beach is right next to the hotel.

And Mother can't leave her curlers at home, or Father's pajamas, or Mother's robe, or Mother's slippers with the silk tassels.

Father is the only one who sits in the cafeteria in suit and tie. But Mother wouldn't want it any other way.

Dinner is ready on the table, it's steaming and steaming, and the waitress is friendly to Father again, and that's definitely not coincidental. And Mother's face is wilting, Mother's nose is dripping. Mother's neck vein is swelling, Mother's hair falls into her eyes, Mother's mouth is trembling, Mother is dipping her spoon deep into the soup.

Father shrugs his shoulders, Father keeps looking at the waitress and loses the soup on its way to his mouth, yet purses his lips for the empty spoon and slurps and sticks the spoon into his mouth up to the handle. Father is sweating on his forehead.

And before you know it the little one has spilled the glass. The water is dripping to the floor through Mother's dress, before you know it he's stuck his spoon into his shoe, before you know it he's torn up the flowers from the vase and scattered them on the green salad.

Father is at the end of his patience, Father's eyes turn milky and ice cold, and Mother's eyes turn large and hot. He's your child too, after all, just as he's mine. Mother, Father, and the little one walk by the beer counter.

Father slows down, and Mother says that beer is out of the question, no, absolutely not.

And Father hates that child that got a crimson sunburn the very first day. And Mother's shuffling walk follows him. He knows without turning that those shoes are too tight for her too, that her flesh swells over the edges, just as with all the other ones, that there aren't any shoes in this world that are wide enough for her feet, for her little toe that is always crooked and sore and bandaged.

Mother is dragging the child beside her and mumbles to herself a sentence that is as long as the road, that waitresses are whores, rotten creatures, miserable things that don't get anywhere in this world. The child cries and drags along and falls to the ground, and the traces of Mother's fingers are more bright red on his cheeks than his sunburn.

Mother can't find the key to the room and turns her purse upside down, and Father finds her greasy wallet disgusting, her money always crumpled up, her sticky comb, her handkerchiefs that are always wet.

Finally they find the keys in Father's coat pocket, and Mother's eyes get wet, Mother's body bends and she cries.

And the light flickers, and the door jams, and the elevator gets stuck. Father forgets the child in the elevator. Mother pounds on the door of the room with both hands.

In the afternoon it's nap time.

Father is sweating and snoring, Father is lying on his tummy, Father is burying his face and in his dream he leaves spit stains on his pillow. The child is tugging at the blanket, digging with his feet, he frowns and in his dream says the poem he recited at the final celebrations in preschool. Mother is lying awake and rigid under the badly washed sheets, under the badly painted ceiling, behind the badly washed windows. Her knitting is on the chair.

Mother is knitting an arm. Mother is knitting a back, Mother is knitting a collar, Mother knits a button hole into the collar.

Mother writes a postcard: Here you can see the hotel where we are staying. I marked our window with a little *x*. The other *x* down there in the sand shows where we always take our sunbaths.

We always go there early in the morning so that we are first and nobody can take our place.

THE STREET SWEEPERS

The town is steeped in emptiness.

A car's lights run over my eyes.

The driver curses because he couldn't see me in the dark.

The street sweepers are at work.

They sweep out the light bulbs, they sweep the streets out of the town, they sweep the living out of the houses, they sweep thoughts out of my head, they sweep me from one leg to the other, they sweep the steps out of my walk.

The street sweepers are sending their brooms after me, their jumping skinny brooms. Clattering, my shoes drop from my body.

I walk behind me, I fall out of myself, over the edge of my imagination.

The park near me barks. The owls eat the kisses left on the benches. The owls ignore me. Tired, strained dreams are cowering in the bushes.

The brooms brush off my back because I am leaning too heavily into the night.

The street sweepers heap up the stars with their brooms, they sweep them onto their shovels and empty them into the canal.

One street sweeper calls something to another street sweeper, and that one to another, and that one again to another one.

Now all the street sweepers of all the streets are talking in a jumble. I walk through their cries, through the foam of their outbursts, I break apart, I fall into depths of meanings.

I walk in great strides. I tear my legs out walking.

The street is swept away.

The brooms attack me.

Everything tumbles over.

The town roams across the fields, going somewhere or other.

BLACK PARK

Sitting in the apartment building, sitting in a block of stone and listening to how the wind tears at the doors and listening just because the door doesn't close.

Forever believing that someone is coming, and then it's nighttime and too late for that visit.

Forever watching how the curtain bulges as if a huge ball were coming into the room.

The flowers in the vases are such big bouquets that they are thickets, beautiful and in disarray, as if they were lives.

And so much trouble you have with this life.

Stepping over bottles that are still there on the rug from last night. The closet door wide open, clothes are lying in it like in a tomb. So empty, as if their owner didn't exist.

Autumn for the dogs in the park, for the late weddings in the summer gardens in November, with borrowed money and big blazing red flowers and toothpicks in the olives.

Everywhere brides in rented cars, the city full of photographers with plaid hats. Their film tears behind the brides' dresses.

Blue-eyed wrinkled girl, where are you going on so much asphalt so early in the morning? Year after year through the black park.

When you said summer is coming you didn't think of summer.

And what are you saying about fall as if this city were not made of stone, as if a single leaf ever wilted on it.

Your friends have shadows in their hair and watch how sad you are and get used to it and resign themselves to it. That's the way you are. What can be done when whatever we say we talk about loss. Is there any hope when the fear in the wine glasses helps with fear and when the bottle gets emptier and emptier.

When laughter becomes guffawing, when they bend with laughter, when they die with laughter, is there any hope? And yet we are so young.

And a dictator has been overthrown again, and the Mafia has killed someone again, and a terrorist is dying in Italy.

You can't drink away your fear, girl. You are sipping from this glass like all those women who don't have a life, who don't fit in with all that trash. Not even their own.

Your friends say, things will go badly for you, girl.

Your eyes are empty. Your feeling is empty and stale. It's a pity about you, girl, it's a pity.

For Richard

WORKDAY

Seven-thirty in the morning. The alarm rings.

I get up, take off my dress, put it on the pillow, put on my pajamas, go to the kitchen, get into the bathtub, take the towel, wash my face with it, take the comb, dry myself with it, take the toothbrush, comb my hair with it, take the sponge, brush my teeth with it. Then I go to the bathroom, eat a slice of tea, and drink a cup of bread.

I take off my wristwatch and my rings.

I take off my shoes.

I go out to the staircase, then I open the apartment door.

I take the elevator from the fifth to the first floor.

Then I walk up nine flights of stairs and find myself in the street.

In the food store I buy a newspaper, then I go to the streetcar stop and buy myself some rolls, and when I arrive at the newspaper stand I get into the streetcar.

Three stops before getting on I get off.

I answer the greeting of the doorman, then the doorman greets me and says, here it's Monday again and again a week is over.

I enter the office, say good-bye, hang my jacket on the desk, sit down at the coat rack, and start working. I work for eight hours.

AFTERWORD

Herta Müller was born in 1953 in the Banat region, a German-language "island" in Romania. Most of the German-speaking people in this area originated in Swabia. Müller studied German and initially worked as a translator and German teacher. *Nadirs (Niederungen)* was her first book. Its successful publication in 1982 in Romania and its highly acclaimed publication with Rotbuch Verlag in Germany in 1984 enabled her to continue working as a freelance writer. She has lived in Germany since 1987.

Müller has been one of the most prolific and acclaimed writers of the last decade. Rainer Moritz expresses many critics' opinions when he says about her writing, "How ridiculous those sweeping lamentations over the decline of contemporary literature are" (*Rheinischer Merkur*, 7 March, 1994; my translation).

Müller has received several prestigious prizes, including the $140,000 International IMPAC Dublin Literary Award (1998). Among other important prizes are the "aspekte" Literaturpreis for *Niederungen* in 1984, the Marie Luise Fleisser Prize and the Ricarda Huch Prize in 1989, and the Kleist Prize in 1994. In worthy memory of Heinrich von Kleist, a nineteenth-century writer ahead of his time, Müller titled her acceptance speech "Von der gebrechlichen Einrichtung der Welt." While the words here are somewhat ambivalent, they could be translated as: "About the fragile nature of this world." And that seems to be a dominant feeling for both writers.

Müller's writing is built on seemingly naive and simple details that suddenly reveal an abyss. Her language art arose from living as a member of a minority in Romania. It is marked by a sense of alienation in a setting that is both privately and publicly oppressive.

The oppressive state is the underlying theme in Müller's prose, but she shows this oppression and the repressions arising from it in individual lives. The latent violence and corruption in the home become symbolic for the conditions in the country, and the silence of her parents represents the human repressions in society in general.

Nadirs deals with the bleak world of Müller's childhood. The book does not have a plot in any conventional sense. It is a collection of a child's often nightmarish impressions of life in her village. Reality and the fantastic, often dreamlike images are mixed in a seamless way to produce visions that present the inner life of the child rather than "realistic" descriptions. The title not only refers to the geographical location of lowlands, but also reflects the oppressive atmosphere that overwhelms the child. Müller has found imaginative expression for the horror in her life. And while she tells stories of her particular village, the conditions and images have universal appeal.

I want to thank a particularly talented group of students in my Techniques of Translation class for valuable suggestions in the revision process. They are Cassandra Garcia, Susan Knudten, Leah Krebs, and especially Ellen Stuart.

Sieglinde Lug
University of Denver